ELEPHANT GOLD

Eric Campbell has spent most of his working life in the tropics, mainly in Papua New Guinea, where he lived at the foot of an active volcano for nine years, and in East Africa, where he lived in the shadow of Mount Kilimanjaro.

He now lives in North Yorkshire with his family.

ELEPHANT GOLD

ERIC CAMPBELL

MACMILLAN CHILDREN'S BOOKS

First published 1997 by Macmillan Children's Book
This edition published 1997 by Macmillan Children's Books
a division of Macmillan Publishers Limited
25 Eccleston Place, London SW1W 9NF
and Basingstoke

Associated companies throughout the world

ISBN 0 330 34728

1 3 5 7 9 8 6 4 2

A CIP catalogue record for this book is available from
the British Library.

Phototypeset by Intype London Ltd
Printed by Mackays of Chatham plc, Kent

For my wife, Judith, without whom no books
would have been written.

ACKNOWLEDGEMENTS

Isak Dinesen: lines from *Out of Africa*, first published in Great Britain 1937 by The Bodley Head. Reproduced by kind permission of Florence Feiler, Literary Agent, Los Angeles, California.

Iain and Oria Douglas-Hamilton: lines from *Among the Elephants*, first published in Great Britain by William Collins Sons & Co. Ltd, 1975. Reproduced by kind permission of The Harvill Press.

T.S. Eliot: lines from 'East Coker' (*Collected Poems 1909–1962*). Reproduced by kind permission of Faber and Faber Ltd.

Elspeth Huxley: lines from *The Mottled Lizard*, first published in Great Britain by Chatto and Windus Ltd, 1962. Reproduced by kind permission of Random House UK Ltd.

Peter Matthiessen: lines from *The Tree Where Man Was Born*, first published in the United States 1972 by E.P. Dutton and Co. Inc., New York. First published in Great Britain by William Collins Sons & Co. Ltd, 1989. Copyright © *The New Yorker* 1972. Reproduced by kind permission of The Harvill Press.

Cynthia Moss: lines from *Elephant Memories*, first published in Great Britain 1976 by Hamish Hamilton, copyright © 1975, 1982, 1989 by Cynthia Moss. Reproduced by permission of Penguin UK.

Baroness Orczy: lines from *The Scarlet Pimpernel* (1905). Reproduced by kind permission of A.P. Watt Ltd on behalf of Sara Orczy-Barstow Brown.

Heathcote Williams: lines from *Sacred Elephant*, first published in Great Britain 1989 by Jonathan Cape Ltd. Reproduced by kind permission of Random House UK Ltd.

W.B. Yeats: lines from 'The Second Coming' (*Collected Poems of W.B. Yeats*). Reproduced by kind permission of A.P. Watt Ltd on behalf of Michael Yeats.

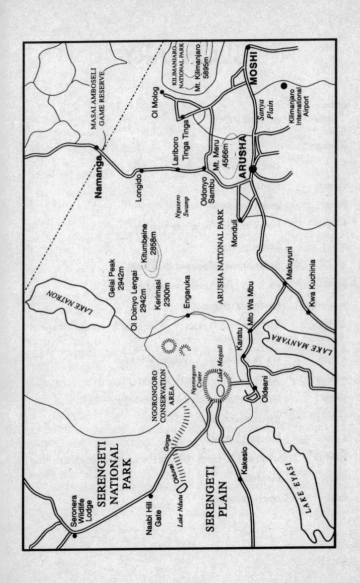

GLOSSARY

Maasai	
Chagga	African tribes
Bantu	
Kamba	
boma	stock corral, usually thorn fenced
bwana	mister/sir
donga	gully/ravine
habari	how's things?/how are you?
jambo	hello
jangili	professional elephant poachers
kopje	rock outcrop/small isolated hill
manyatta	fenced settlement
Mchawi	literally 'witch doctor'. The man in charge of spells for the *jangili*
morani	warrior (Maasai); (plural: *il-moran*)
mzungu	white person; (plural: *wazungu*)
panga	large, broad-bladed knife, machete
shamba	garden/farm plot
shifta	bandit (Somali)
sjambok	whip made from rhinoceros or hippopotamus hide
tembo	elephant
veldt	open grassland

'Then came the great elephant . . . the wise elephant.'

Bestiary, Harleian Manuscript 3244, British Museum, circa AD 1250

ONE

'There is not any creature so capable of understanding as an Elephant. They are apt to learne, remember, meditate and conceive such things as a man can hardly perform.'

Edward Topsell, *The History of Four-Footed Beasts*, 1607

We are what our memories make us.

Events, great and small, change us. Nothing we experience goes to waste. Nothing is ever truly forgotten. Memories are always there, stored at the back of the brain, waiting for a trigger to retrieve them.

So, although time eased the hurt, dulled the fear and the horror and the grief, the memory of that day remained with him throughout his long life – ever-present, ever instantly evokable in vivid clarity.

The memory moulded his ways, directed him along all the paths of his days.

They were walking across open country, about twenty of them in single file. There was no urgency, no hurry. When he and the other young ones needed to rest, everyone stopped and waited for them. Then, when they were ready, they started to move again.

He didn't know where they were going and had no need to know. He simply walked beside his mother, shielded from the hot morning sun by her shadow, protected, as he always had been, by her and by all the other adults with their communal knowledge of the land and its dangers.

The group walked almost without sound. The ground was soft and yielding after the rains and their feet made only the faintest sluffings as they brushed through the sweet-smelling new grasses. Now and then the silence of the great plain would be broken by a far-off bark or grunt of warning as distant, ever-watchful animals noticed their approach, assessed them for threat and moved discreetly out of their path.

As the sun crept up the sky towards its zenith, the heat began to sap their energy. Eventually their leader turned them off the path and headed them for a small clump of trees nestling in the lee of a low hill. As they approached the copse, the leader signalled them to wait and went on alone.

They stood in silence until she had satisfied herself that there was no danger then, on her call, they moved forward to join her. The single line fragmented now, as individuals, or small groups of mothers and children, entered the copse at different points.

The shade gave immediate relief from the burning sun but, strangely, his mother did not stop to take advantage of it, continuing through the trees without pausing.

They emerged on the other side of the trees at the top of a small slope which dropped down to the base of the hill. Here the rains had collected in a wide, semi-circular depression and formed a crystal-clear lake which shone blindingly in the noon sun.

Delighted, he trotted down the slope and knelt at the lake's edge, drinking gratefully. The other youngsters followed, some tentatively, unsure whether to leave their mothers, some, more

2

confident, careering headlong down the hillside and plunging, joyously, straight into the water. The adults followed more sedately but were no less glad to sink into the coolness and ease the burning of their skins and throats. Soon the entire group was lost in the pleasure of it all as they rolled and splashed and cavorted.

There was noise.

Much noise.

That was the fatal, tragic component of the day. The noise.

Without the noise they might have heard the whirring starter-motors of the phalanx of dark-green Land Rovers drawn up in formation on the other side of the hill. Might have heard them grind slowly round the back of the hill and re-form into a deadly, lethal barrier in front of the trees. Have heard the click of door catches. The footfalls and whispered voices. The terrible, metallic clunk of magazines of heavy bullets engaging into semi-automatic rifles.

Without the noise they might have escaped.

As it was, death came out of nowhere.

The men emerged from the trees and onto the top of the slope without being noticed. The first gun was raised to the shoulder without any of them seeing it.

And then it began.

When the first shot rang out he was, like all the others, still playing happily in the water. He stopped, his attention arrested by the sound. All the others stopped too, as incomprehension silenced and immobilized them.

But the silence lasted only a few seconds. It was broken by a deep, unearthly and terrifying scream of pain and he watched, horrified, as one of the adults shuddered briefly then fell onto her side and writhed, frantically, in the water.

After that he had no idea what was happening, knew only

3

that sudden fear coursed through his body, making him lurch instinctively to his feet.

Instantly the day was transformed into a maelstrom of noise and confusion. The air was cracked apart with an unending stream of thunderous bangings, ripped with the sickening thud of bullets into soft flesh, torn with the harsh, bewildered screams of the dying.

Through the noise he heard his mother calling him and began to run towards the sound. He caught sight of her through a press of bodies but, as he tried to reach her, he was knocked flying by one of the mortally wounded adults who was whirling round and round in a mad death-dance. He staggered to his feet again, but the fall had winded him and he stopped briefly to catch his breath. His mother began to run towards him but suddenly, inexplicably, stopped and became very still. She remained completely motionless for long seconds. Then, horrified, he watched as her legs simply buckled beneath her and she crashed down into the water. He ran up to her and pushed at her, screaming for her to get up.

She did not move.

Then it all became too much. The noise and the horror, the smell of blood and the writhing of the wounded, the screams of the dying and the sheer, nightmare unreality numbed his senses.

Instinct took over.

'Run,' instinct said. 'RUN.'

He spun away from it all.

He had no idea which way to run, no idea from where the danger came. He just ran, panic driving his legs.

It was purely chance, not choice, that took him back up the slope, back the way they had come. Others had tried this way too, but by now he was beyond registering anything and did not even notice the bleeding bodies that he passed.

He did not know it, but he was running directly into the

4

line of men. Probably he would not have turned away even if he had known. There was nothing in his mind now but the urgency of running, of escape.

He came to the top of the rise and headed for the trees. So confused was his poor, harried mind that the men ranged in front of the copse did not register until he was almost upon them. When he did finally see them, it was only as brief, blurred shapes as they scattered before him, jumping frantically out of his blundering path.

Perhaps he did not even see the small, heavily built, bearded man who stood his ground, gun raised to his shoulder, or hear the high whine of the bullet as it whooshed past his head.

Probably he did not even feel the thud as he hit the man head-on, flinging him to the ground like a rag doll, or hear the crunch of bone and the man's agonized scream as he was trampled.

Only later, when the deep cuts carved into his mind by the events of this day had healed into scars, would he remember.

And remember

And remember.

We are what our memories make us.

TWO

'In 1986 the number of elephants killed to supply
the United States market for worked ivory
amounted to 32,254. And 75 per cent of that
year's imports were declared as originating in
African countries which had prohibited ivory
exports – making them illegal imports under the
Lacey Act.'

*Petition to Upgrade the African Elephant from Threatened to
Endangered Status*, Washington, DC: The International
Wildlife Coalition, December 1988

Hyram T. Johnson,
202 San Angelo Court,
Queens,
New York.
20 May

M. Taylor
P.O. Box 922,
Arusha,
Tanzania,
East Africa.

Dear Taylor,
Greetings!

How's the safari business? Gullible tourists like me still paying big bucks for you to insult them and get them lost, or has the word spread?

Want to know something interesting? There was this smash on Brooklyn Bridge last week. 'Big deal' I hear you say from the depths of Serengeti. Well, shut up and listen.

This kamikaze cab smashes into this truck, see, and knocks it onto its side. No one's hurt, but the road's blocked, so obviously someone's going to wake up one of our useless city cops – if they can find one – to sort the mess out.

Keep listening!

Before the cops arrive, this truck driver gets out and starts throwing these big parcels into the goddamn river. So, we're all crazy in New York and who cares?

You still listening? Here's the interesting bit.

By coincidence, a couple of days later these police frogmen are down there searching for some poor jerk

8

who's thrown himself off the bridge and they find these parcels and bring 'em up.

Want to know what's in 'em?

Only elephant tusks, that's what.

Listening now, aren't you?

So, what'll happen? Nothing. Zilch'll happen. The police are 'interviewing' the driver. That's cop-speak for putting the screws on until someone gets frightened and coughs up a big bribe and the whole thing gets forgotten. They're all bent.

But I ain't forgotten that day on Serengeti when we came on them goddamn poachers and them poor goddamn elephants and I ain't forgetting this.

I'm going into the Private Investigator business for a day or two. The truck's owned by some Chinese guy called Tommy Cheung. He's got a shop in Manhattan selling Chinese furniture and the like.

The guy's going to get a little visit.

I'll be in touch.

Regards,

Hyram

P.S. Here's fifty bucks for that poor devil Benny. He deserves some compensation having to drive for a schmuck like you.

TAYLOR'S TOURS
P.O. Box 922, Arusha, East Africa. Tel: Arusha 5782.

6 June

Dear Hyram,

Oh no, I thought I'd heard the last of you.

It's all very interesting, but what do you want me to do? I'm trying to run a business here, though with the amount of trouble 'clients' like you cause it's hardly worth it. I can't mount guard on the entire world's elephant population as well. So someone's smuggling ivory. Tell me something I don't know.

Yours,

Mike Taylor

P.S. If you're thinking of coming back for another safari I'm fully booked for the next two hundred years.

P.P.S. Benny thanks you for the $50. He spent it on a cassette player for the Land Rover. In about two days I intend to shoot it.

M. Taylor,
P.O. Box 922,
Arusha.

Dear Taylor,

Thanks for your letter. Glad to see you're still sweet-tempered and co-operative!

Want to know something interesting?

I got arrested, that's what. Not before time, some might say. Anyway I'm out on $2000 bail.

Jeez! We got a million psychopaths in New York and they arrest me.

Here's what happened.

I go down to Manhattan one night and find this guy Cheung's shop. It's all technicolor carpets and big carved chests and junk like that. A few ivory ornaments about, but not much. So I hang around till about 2 a.m. then go round the back and break in. There's this little window I get through, which ain't no fun my size.

Anyway I'm in and looking round this guy's office and thinking about getting some of the files down off the shelves when I hear this police siren and figure that the shop's got one of those alarms that goes off down in the cop-station and decide perhaps I'll leave. But the door's got this goddamn deadlock, see, and I can't open it and I'm climbing headfirst out the goddamn window again and I'm half in and half out

11

when the cops arrive and say 'Ah, Mr. Houdini I presume' and witty stuff like that and throw me in the slammer for the night.

'So,' I hear you say, 'a complete failure.'

Not quite!

As I'm leaving I pick up the only thing to hand. On the guy's desk is one of those flip-up telephone number files so I grab this and when I'm half in and half out the window and not wishing to get caught with it I lob it into a trash can in the alley before the cops arrive. I know it's safe there because being New York they only collect the garbage once every century.

I've been back for it!

There's a lot of numbers and names. They're all U.S. or Hong Kong numbers, which figures, and ain't no interest to us – apart from one. Here it is!

Laurens van der Wel. Moshi 6471.

Moshi, Tanzania.

So, you tell me – they got Chinese furniture factories in Tanzania now?

I'm jumping bail. I got a flight gets into Kilimanjaro Airport Sunday at 8 a.m.

Pick me up. I ain't riding in no goddamn Tanzanian taxis!

Regards,

Hyram

P.S. Benny – here's 200 bucks. Bribe whoever needs bribing and get all the 'petroli' you can.

THREE

'Go to Africa to heal the heart.'

Anon.

The plane touched down at Kilimanjaro airport just after eight o'clock on a humid but brilliant morning.

Emerging from the air-conditioned comfort of the huge jet's interior, Hyram Johnson swore quietly to himself.

'Jeez,' he muttered, as the heat and sodden air took his breath away.

He stopped at the foot of the aircraft steps, allowing his body a moment to adjust to the violence of the temperature. The ground was still wet from overnight rain and it steamed gently under the growing heat of the morning sun. A warm breeze blew in from the southern Maasai Steppe. It swirled the steam around the passengers' legs as they passed by him and walked towards the terminal building.

'Jeez,' Hyram said again. 'At my age I should know better. Ten thousand kilometres for a sauna bath. I need my head examined. I just hope that schmuck Taylor hasn't forgotten me.'

Perspiration was already beginning to run down his forehead and into his eyes, blinding him. He pulled a handkerchief from his pocket and wiped the irritation away.

He sighed.

The exhaustion of the long flight dampened any excitement he might have felt about being back in Africa and he gave only a perfunctory glance around before heaving his heavy shoulder bag into place and moving along with the stream of people heading for the horrors of Customs and Immigration.

There was nothing much to see anyway. The great volcanic peaks of Kilimanjaro and Meru which, on a clear day, make this airport the most spectacular and magical entrance in all of Africa, were both shrouded in heavy, low cloud. Beyond the airport fence the steppe stretched away to infinity, featureless and empty in every direction. The huge, once elegantly beautiful, terminal building had, over the years, fallen into shabby decay, its paint stripped inexorably away by the merciless sun. Built with high hopes of welcoming hordes of free-spending tourists bringing precious income to one of the poorest countries in the world, it had been a failure. The tourists had mostly gone elsewhere and the airport, isolated in the Maasai Steppe, far from any town, had become a forlorn anachronism, dispiriting even before you entered it.

By the time Hyram reached the Immigration desk he was at the back of the queue and there were already fierce arguments going on. The loudest of these attracted his attention. A large, important-looking

African was bellowing at an unimpressed clerk. Hyram listened and smiled.

The man had no visa for Tanzania and could not enter the country. The clerk was politely apologetic, but adamant that there was no way round this problem. No matter that the man was a personal friend of the Finance Minister; no matter that he was an important government official himself, on his way home to Zimbabwe, but with important business to transact here; he had no visa and that was that. He must re-board the plane and continue to Harare.

Hyram knew it was all show. He had been coming to Tanzania long enough to recognize this for what it was — a well-rehearsed charade in which the actors were all aware of their respective roles. When the required posturings were over, money would change hands and the man would be allowed in. Everyone knew that. Everyone understood the system, but enjoyed the ritual protestations.

Hyram knew that he would be refused entry too. The officials would be quick to spot that his Yellow Fever vaccination was out of date, but there was already a $20 bill inside his health certificate which he hoped would induce a temporary blindness. If he got into real trouble no doubt Taylor would ease his path.

If the schmuck had turned up.

In the event he had no trouble at all. The dollars vanished by sleight of hand, winks were given to the Customs Officers, who smilingly chalked crosses on his bags, and he was through and into the Arrivals Lounge.

It was empty. No Taylor.

'Damn him,' Hyram snarled vehemently under his breath.

He walked over to the big, plate-glass exit doors and scanned up and down the road, searching for the battered white Land Rover.

Nothing.

'I might have known. He's probably two hundred kilometres away, sitting under a tree drinking a cold beer.'

He decided not to brave the chaos outside. Out on the forecourt an intimidating army of ragged taxi-drivers was competing, in deafening tones, for customers to ride to the hotels of Moshi and Arusha in the dilapidated death-traps they called taxis. After twenty hours of aeroplanes and airports that was more than he could stand.

Irritably he selected a chair under the only fan in the building that was working and slumped into it. He would wait until the mêlée was over, then, if Taylor didn't arrive he would make his own way into Arusha, track him down and perhaps, he mused with pleasurable anticipation, strangle him.

Gradually the hubbub from outside began to die down as passengers finished negotiating exorbitant prices for their peril-fraught journeys, climbed into their taxis and were whisked away in loud crashings of tortured gearboxes and great clouds of black smoke from ruined engines.

Soon it was all over.

Briefly the glass in all the doors and windows of the airport vibrated madly as the DC10 hurtled down the runway and took off for Harare. By the time the thunder of its engines was fading the airport was already falling silent.

The baggage handlers climbed onto their bicycles and pedalled off down the long airport entrance road back to their villages.

The Customs men, in their Rolex watches and Ray-Ban sunglasses, climbed into their cars and drove away to gloat over the flight's confiscated goods.

The cleaners listlessly stirred the dust from one place to another then, unable even to afford bicycles, set off down the road on foot.

The day's business was over. That was it.

In this great airport, capable of handling a hundred and fifty flights a day, this one, half-full DC10 was all that would arrive today. Or indeed for several days. Everyone could go home.

And Hyram sat, listening to the weary fan above his head grind slowly round. It was providing no relief at all from the stifling heat. It merely angered the mosquitoes who were gathering around his head, whining with the excitement of finding a source of nourishment. He slapped at them as they settled on his neck. They left tiny black and red smudges on his hands.

He wasn't worried.

In spite of the uncharitable thoughts he had had earlier, he knew that Mike Taylor would turn up in his own good time. Everything Taylor did was at his own pace. He seemed to take a perverse delight in irritating the tourists upon whom his livelihood depended.

Hyram shook his head as he remembered his first

safari with this man, five years ago. The arguments which had developed, the insults traded, the impression Taylor invariably gave that Africa was his own personal country and that tourists, having crawled out from under stones, were deeply unwelcome.

But, in the end, irritating though they had been, those things had not mattered. They had been displaced by darker things. Terrible things which had been burned deep into their minds and which had brought two very difficult, uncompromising men together with a common purpose.

And that was why Hyram knew that Taylor would be here. If there was a chance of bringing an elephant poacher to book then he wouldn't be able to resist it. Hyram knew that his letters would have whetted Taylor's appetite, no matter what protestations he had made.

He'd turn up. Of that Hyram was certain.

And he was right. Two hours passed. Just enough time to make Hyram really angry, but not so much that he would give up and hitch a lift into Arusha. Just the right amount of time to make the point that Taylor was the boss, no matter who was paying for his time.

From where he was sitting Hyram could see the main Arusha-Moshi road about half a mile away. Throughout his wait there was very little traffic; just the odd, ancient truck trailing smoke, or a pick-up so loaded with passengers that its back end nearly scraped the ground.

But, eventually, the white Land Rover he had expected to see came roaring down from Arusha, swung into the airport entrance road on two wheels and grew rapidly in size as it hurtled towards him.

Hyram stood and gathered up his bags.

'Schmuck,' he said.

But he smiled as he said it.

FOUR

'. . . the nearest thing on earth
To a cloud.'

Heathcote Williams, *Sacred Elephant*, 1989

The herd began to move just after dawn. A light mist still swirled wispily above the ground so that the huge, grey shapes, moving with eerie silence, melted into invisibility and then reappeared again, as though great boulders were floating in and out of vision on a pale sea.

The elephants travelled in single file.

A massive female, ancient and wise, led them out of the copse where they had slept. She held her head high and lifted her trunk into a question mark as she sniffed the air for danger. Behind her, six younger cows and an assortment of calves and adolescents followed calmly, knowing the matriarch's great knowledge and experience kept them from harm. At the rear of the column another old, calfless female with huge, curving tusks flapped her ears as she turned her head this way and that. Her acute hearing picked up the soft gonging of Maasai cattle bells. They were far in the distance and posed no threat, but she gave a soft snort to warn the others nevertheless.

Without that snort of warning the occupants of the two small, green tents would have been unaware that the elephants were leaving.

Matthew Blake opened his eyes, reluctantly pulled one arm out of the warmth of his sleeping bag and nudged the amorphous shape lying next to him. The shape groaned.

'What?' it said.

'They're moving.'

Alison Blake's head emerged from her sleeping bag. She looked around blearily and cocked her head to one side, listening.

'I can't hear anything,' she said.

'I once saw this 1940s cowboy film,' her brother replied. 'An old cowboy was giving some advice to a younger one. He said, "If you hears sumpthin – that's nuthin. If you hears nuthin – them's Injuns." For Injuns read elephants. They're moving. I heard Aunt Emily snorting. Come on, let's wake Dad up. Shake a leg.'

Matt dragged himself out of his bag and crawled out through the tent flap. He shivered a little in the cold of the morning and trotted straight over to the Land Rover and got his coat. It would be another hour before the day started to warm and the dank mist began to lift. He climbed up onto the roof of the vehicle and peered round until he caught a glimpse of the line of elephants sliding away through the mist, noting their direction. Then he jumped down, crossed over to the other tent and shook the front pole, causing the whole structure to rattle and flap.

'Dad. They're moving. Time to get up.'

Another muffled groaning and a barely audible grumbling. Matt continued to shake the tent until a voice finally said, 'All right, all right, I heard you the first time. I'm coming.'

Matt grinned and returned to the Land Rover. He opened the back door, turned on the gas of the little camping stove and lit it. He warmed his hands for a second on the bright blue flame, then put the kettle on for some tea.

Alison lay quietly, enjoying the noises of the new day. She smiled to herself, as she had every day for the past week, with the pleasure of waking up in Africa instead of wet, dismal England. The school year had seemed interminable.

She stretched, sighed and immediately put school out of her mind. It was all over anyway, so why think about it? For the next two months she could be where she belonged.

She sat up, unzipped the sleeping bag and started to get dressed. A couple of minutes later she emerged from the tent, yawning and pulling on her sweater. She tied her long, blonde hair back in a pony-tail then went straight over to the Land Rover.

'Time?' she demanded, picking up the heavy diary from the front seat.

'Six forty-five.'

'Right. Direction?'

'South-westish. Towards Lengai. I think they may be heading for the swamp.'

Alison flicked through the pages of the book until she came to the first blank one.

'Twenty-seventh of June, if you didn't know,' she

announced as she recorded the information at the top of the page.

'I know. You don't have to keep telling us the date,' Matt grinned. 'We haven't forgotten your birthday's in a few days. Though I don't know that "sweet" sixteen is going to sum you up.'

Alison flicked her head back with annoyance.

'Stupid,' she snapped. 'I'm not telling you for that reason. It's Cleopatra. She's huge. You saw her when she settled down to sleep last night. She couldn't get comfortable at all, and all the others were flapping around her like fussy old midwives. I think she'll give birth today. If it's a male I might call him Anthony.'

'We'll call it "Five-thirteen", whatever it is,' said an irritable voice from the tent. 'I don't approve of all this naming. It's not scientific. Give an animal a name and you give it a character, by association. The calf will be number thirteen in herd five. That's all.'

'Oh Dad,' Alison replied, sighing.

She looked at her brother and rolled her eyes with exasperation. This was a long-running, daily argument.

'You've got it the wrong way round. They don't assume characters because of their names. I give them names because of their characters. Cleopatra's called that because she's so beautiful. She has huge eye-lashes that she flutters and all the bulls adore her. You use your boring old numbers if you want. It's your study. I can't think of them as numbers.'

'Flutters her eyelashes, eh?' said the voice from the tent. There was a brief rustling and John Blake's head appeared through the tent flap, grinning. He looked affectionately at his daughter.

'That's a very scientific observation,' he added. 'I'm

sure the Research Institute will be very interested in that.'

'If they're not they ought to be,' Alison retorted, tossing her head back imperiously.

'The kettle's boiling,' said Matt. 'Stop arguing, come and get some tea and let's get on the road. If she is going to give birth it'll be the first interesting thing to happen since they saw off those lionesses two weeks ago. It would be just like us to miss the great event.'

'Well, that's research,' John Blake said, as he emerged from the tent and stretched. 'Long periods of waiting for something big to happen. Just like life really.'

He took the mug of steaming tea that Matt was holding out for him and went to sit on the bonnet of the Land Rover to drink it. Alison helped herself to tea then turned to walk back towards the tent. She stopped after a couple of paces.

'Er, Matt,' she said nervously.

'What?'

'Take a look.'

Without any of them noticing, a huge grey baboon had slipped silently into their camp and was squatting outside Matt and Alison's tent. He sat fatly, his stomach rolling in folds like a portly old gentleman, watching them with expectant interest.

John Blake glanced round.

'Oh, it's only Esau,' he called. 'He's taken to calling round for breakfast. He's getting old and idle, I think. Knows where there's a free meal.'

The baboon scratched his dog-like head and yawned widely, revealing ferocious teeth in massively powerful jaws.

'Throw him a couple of those old sausages out of the cold-box. That'll keep him happy. They're going bad anyway.'

Matt reached into the box, walked a little way towards the baboon and lobbed the sausages at him. Esau fielded them dexterously and started to nibble at them with surprising delicacy.

Alison watched warily.

'Is he dangerous?'

'No, not Esau. I've known him for years. He makes a bit of a nuisance of himself climbing into Safari Companies' buses and ransacking the tourists' bags, but that's all. He's never attacked anyone to my knowledge. The tourists don't know that, of course. When Esau climbs in, the tourists leave quite quickly. Sometimes head first through the windows. For some strange reason that endears him to me.'

'Haven't I read that baboons are vegetarian?' Alison asked.

Esau chewed his sausages happily, quite unconcerned by the accusation.

'Probably,' Matt answered. 'Nobody's told Esau though.'

Alison furrowed her brow, then turned and addressed her father.

'So it's "Esau", is it? Aren't you the man who just gave me a lecture on naming animals?'

'Ah, but that's different. He's an old friend. And we're not studying baboons, we're studying elephants. That's a big difference. In fact sometimes I think Esau's studying us. I wonder what he makes of us all?'

Alison looked at Matt and shook her head. It was no good continuing. They had long ago come to accept that there was no logic about their father, scientist or not. An illogical scientist was a contradiction in terms but they had learned to live with it in an exasperated fashion.

'Right,' said Matt, putting an end to the discussion by throwing the remains of his tea onto the ground. 'Let's get the tents down and get on our way. We can have breakfast when the elephants stop to feed, then we can watch them at the same time.'

He clapped his hands hard together several times. 'Breakfast's over, Esau. Go home.'

The baboon got up, curled back his lips, gave a half-hearted chatter of friendly insolence and shuffled off into the trees.

'Friend or not,' Alison observed, 'I wouldn't like to meet him on a dark night.'

Five minutes later they had struck camp, were packed and ready to go.

Matt climbed into his customary position in the driving seat and put the key into the ignition.

Alison, the shortest of the three, climbed in the passenger side door and shuffled across into the middle seat, putting one leg each side of the transmission tunnel.

John Blake got into the passenger seat and made preparations for the day's recordings. He fastened his clipboard into the rack on the dash and clipped his video camera securely into its brackets on the tray fixed to the outside of the door.

'OK Matt,' he said. 'Ready.'

Matt started the engine, swung the big machine round and began to creep slowly and quietly through the bush.

Moments later they emerged onto the hillside and looked out over the plain.

The soft morning sun flooded onto the distant, misted, volcanic peaks. Kerimasi. Kitumbeine. Gelai. Ancient cones floating in a sea of light. Pink and white mirages at the edges of the world.

At their feet a vast, black lake of wildebeest flowed westwards, a million or more animals on the move, eternally seeking something. Or perhaps nothing.

About a kilometre away, the departing herd of elephants whispered silently, like a grey cloud, across the ground. Zebra and antelope skittered and bounced out of their way. Bateleur eagles, high black dots glued, entirely motionless, on a powder-blue sky, watched dispassionately.

In the distance a solitary lion barked a greeting.

John Blake leaned back in his seat and yawned.

'Another boring day at the office,' he said.

FIVE

'If the annual ivory harvest continues, it will eliminate the elephants in eight to ten years.'

Independent, April 1988

The man crossing the dusty compound and making his way between the big wooden sheds was in his seventieth year, though few who observed him would have known it.

True, his hair and beard were bleached pure white, his face deeply lined and burned walnut by a lifetime of exposure to the tropical sun, but his bearing was that of a much younger man.

Short and heavily muscled, he carried himself erect, moved with a strong precision and, to a distant viewer, seemed to exude power and solidity.

The type of man who would not be easily hurt. Who rode whatever blows life dealt him.

A self-contained man. An indestructible man.

But only from a distance.

Closer inspection would reveal that the bearing and the determined tread were achieved at great cost.

The man had a defect that he strove hard to conceal and whose concealment cost him pain at every step.

He limped. Badly.

His right leg was withered and bent, the muscles wasted into knotted strings, the kneecap pushed askew.

Close to, you would see that the leg was so damaged it hardly functioned at all. To walk, the man would place his good leg forward then, with a rolling sway of his whole body, heave the useless limb up off the ground and swing it from the hip. He would grunt with pain from the twisting of his spine and his heavy boot would thud, uncontrolled, to the ground, raising a small cloud of dust as it scuffed along the earth.

Those in the sheds, hearing footsteps approach, would always know it was him. A soft sluffing of one boot, followed by the heavy thump of the other.

Sher-*thunk*. Sher-*thunk*. Sher-*thunk*.

'Ssssss,' they would hiss in warning. '*Bwana* comes. *Bwana* comes.'

If they were idle, they would quickly find a task and bend to it with rapt determination and smile and call out '*Jambo bwana, habari?*' and be the perfect worker.

For if *bwana* found you idle then his rage was unbounded. The *sjambok* would whistle and lay open a cut in your back, your shoulder, your neck or your cheek, slicing clean as any knife wound.

But with twice the pain.

Bwana was almost always displeased. It is a truth that in some people infirmity brings forth light, in others darkness. This man's spirit was as hideously twisted as his leg. Early in life he had come to hate it. To hate its desiccated brittleness, its tortured shape, its bitter uselessness. At first he had tried to hide it from

30

the curious stares of others, but had soon found that though the leg itself could be concealed from watching eyes, its uselessness could not. The sway, the clumsy, rolling walk could not be hidden, no matter how he tried.

And though the eyes that watched him held no scorn, he found it in them anyway. He heard cruel laughter in a silent room, saw mockery on a smiling face. The barest glance of interest would enrage him.

Shame at his deformity ate into him.

Feeling himself a freak, he eventually became one. Friends avoided him and drifted away. People tired of his ill temper, his constant complaints and snarls, his self-pity. He became a man alone, embittered and vengeful.

Above all, *vengeful*.

And here, housed in the dark sheds between which he walked, was his revenge.

He reached the first of them, swung open the big double doors and stepped inside. Light flooded onto a large wooden table where a tall, black figure was at work, methodically scraping a bright square of metal along the surface of an object stretched out on the table. The figure jumped nervously and backed away from the table as the older man swayed into the room.

The older man noticed his movement and immediately sensed that something was wrong.

Sensed fear.

'What?' he snarled.

'Nothing, *bwana*, nothing,' the Somali replied.

But his eyes told a different story. They shifted from side to side as though he sought escape.

'Nothing, eh? We'll see.'

The man limped up to the table, bent over it and closely, minutely, inspected the work. He took a long time. The Somali's fear became tangible, hung on the air.

Finding nothing at first, the man looked closer and began to stroke his fingers softly along the work, seeking out imperfection. Knowing that fault was there.

Finally he picked the object up, limped back to the door and held it up to the light.

The bright morning sun flooded onto it, burnishing it to a vivid tapestry of colour. Whites melted into yellows, yellows into golds. Golds flowed into browns so profound they seemed almost black. The ends of the hairs of the pelt caught the light and danced it back to the eye, so the liquid colours seemed to run, to flow, beneath a sheen of opaque silver.

A thing of startling beauty, of soft perfection.

He stretched the skin out, pulling it taut, and held it up to the sun.

This was the test that proved him right. Almost in the middle of the skin a faint, small line of sunlight shone through.

The skin was damaged. It was cut.

There was total silence for long seconds as the man's anger welled up. Quietly he crumpled the skin in his hands, rolled it into a ball and turned. His pale, watery eyes moved slowly until they rested, finally, on the quivering Somali.

The eyes were cold and rage-filled.

'Sooo . . .' he hissed. The long, drawn-out sibilance of a snake about to strike.

'So . . . now we see what you have done.'

His voice was soft, emotionless, but charged — electric with threat.

'*See what you have done,*' he hissed again, beginning to move forward. He held the balled skin in one hand.

His voice was rising in pitch as anger constricted his throat.

'See!' he screamed.

His arm swung back and, with one ferocious movement, he hurled the skin at the now cowering Somali.

'The skin is cut, you swine. You knew it!'

Limping forward as he spoke, he picked up his *sjambok* from the table. He raised it high as he advanced.

The tall, black man seemed now to have shrunk as he hunched himself back, fearfully, against the wall.

'No, *bwana*. Please. I did not do it, *bwana*. The skin was damaged when I began. Those who caught him damaged him. Not me, *bwana*. A thorn tore the skin, *bwana*. Not me.'

He was almost whimpering now.

'Liar! Filthy liar!'

The arm swung down and the *sjambok* flashed through the air. The Somali threw up his arms to protect his face, but was not quite in time. The cruel leather bit deeply into his forearm, then deflected down onto his face. A vivid weal appeared, with frightening suddenness, on the man's arm and the tip of the *sjambok* caught him just above the eye, slicing a two-inch long fissure in his forehead. Blood began to trickle into the man's eye and down his cheek.

'The skin is ruined, fool. Ruined!'

The *sjambok* descended again. The Somali screamed in pain.

'How many times must I tell you? Scrape the skins softly. *Softly!*'

The *sjambok* snapped down again.

Again the Somali screamed.

'Do you know, fool, how much money you have lost me?'

The *sjambok* descended.

'Two . . .'

The *sjambok*. The pain.

'Thousand . . .'

The *sjambok*. The scream.

'Dollars.'

Again and again the *sjambok* lashed down until the Somali could take no more. Rolling over to one side he escaped the blows, lurched dizzily to his feet and ran, unsteady and howling, from the shed. He fled away across the compound, the blood from his deep wounds spotting the ground, his voice, crying his anguish, diminishing in the distance.

Gasping from his exertions and his anger, the older man leant heavily against the table to draw breath. Small patches of dried blood and parchment-thin slivers of membrane lay on its surface from where the last remaining vestiges of the animal's life had been scraped from its skin.

He glared at the leopard pelt lying where he had thrown it and snarled with rage.

In perfect condition it would have fetched three thousand dollars. Now he would be lucky to get a thousand.

Two thousand dollars lost by one man's careless hand.

He slammed the *sjambok* rhythmically against the table leg, venting his anger.

Thwack. Thwack. Thwack.

Eventually he became calmer and looked around the room, taking in its contents with satisfaction.

The last few weeks' haul had been very good. Stacks of animal skins lined the walls. Zebra, gazelle, Colobus monkey, all neatly tied in bundles of ten so he could count them at a glance.

Zebra. Fifty, a hundred, a hundred and fifty, a hundred and eighty. A good catch. At $100 a skin — $18,000.

His eyes glowed at the thought.

'Eighteen thousand dollars.'

He said it aloud, taking pleasure in hearing it.

But then, of course, there were expenses. Petrol and diesel for the trucks and Land Rovers were scarce again, their purchase difficult and needing heavy bribes.

The bullets, the tools of his trade, had to be bought and were expensive too.

And the men were a worry. Always a worry. Stupid and idle and feckless, they ate into his profit, as this fool had done this morning. But at least with the men he knew they would keep quiet. They were too grateful for the pay he gave them ever to think of reporting his activities.

And too much in fear.

He smiled at the thought of their fear.

Then he remembered what he had come in here for in the first place. Moving away from the table he stumped down to the end of the shed, to where yesterday's prize catch lay under a heavily stained green tarpaulin. Dragging off the cover, he inspected what lay beneath.

His eyes were dispassionate as he scanned the

length of the inert, musty-smelling carcass from black-tipped nose to black-tasselled tail. He searched merely for flaws: for inroads into his profit. If there were any blemishes on this carcass they would be wounds from battles long ago, or the faint scars of healed ulcers. No bullet holes would mar this skin. Bullets were for lesser things, for animals whose pelts would be cut into handbag-sized squares, or the small, delicate strips for fine, ladies' shoes.

Bullets were not for lions. Lions needed to be perfect for their role — to rest, glass-eyed, in flattened death on polished, parquet floors.

He smiled in quiet satisfaction at the thought of all the gold pelts he had supplied adorning smart and pricey flats in London and New York, in Rome and Berlin, in Tokyo and . . . all a world away from Africa.

No, there would be no holes in this one.

This one had taken the dead goat he had left out near the *kopje*. The goat he had carefully, methodically, injected with poison.

This one had died a slow death, but had died the way it mattered — skin intact.

Only the paws were damaged, the claws pulled out, the pads bloodied, as the great beast, frenzied and baffled by its terrible, dying agony had lashed out at rock and tree alike. Lashed out at anything in its insane, final death-dance, hoping it could stop the pain.

The man's eyes saw no beauty as they passed over the animal. They saw only a dead thing, tongue lolling, eyes glazed.

He felt no emotion that the great, easy power that had flowed under this perfect, golden skin was stilled for ever. Felt no pity that the massive black-maned head would no longer raise and roar, with awesome majesty, at vultures pinned against the sky.

Felt no regret, no remorse that a thing of grace was taken from the world.

He saw only profit.

And revenge.

For, in the end, that was what drove him.

Hatred of man, denied an outlet, had transformed gradually to hatred of all living things. Of all things that moved with ease and agility about the world, as he could not. Of all things which came together, lived in harmony and died amongst their kind, as he had been, and would always be, denied. Of all things that loved and had young and were happy.

Of all things that lived lives he could not live.

He threw the tarpaulin roughly back over the carcass and limped back down the length of the shed. He slammed the doors shut and locked them.

Brooding, he swayed across the central clearing to another building.

Here, in this shed, were the most treasured prizes of his revenge.

He unbolted the padlock and eased the doors open.

Sunlight angled in.

This shed was much larger, much longer, its far extremity undiscernible in the dimness. But, though there were no windows, the interior was not dark. Sunlight, seeping through cracks in the walls or the roof, was picked up by the room's contents and reflected, so that the whole building was suffused with a quiet, yellow-white glow. The light was most intense near the doors, where the sun flooded in and was thrown back, dazzlingly, from the rows of tusks stacked neatly and graded by size in racks along the room.

Small tusks, no more than eighteen inches long, were piled on the top racks, down through two-foot, three-foot, five-foot, to the monster eight or nine foot hundred-pounders on the bottom.

Tusks from all ages and sizes of beast.

Hundreds, perhaps thousands, of tusks.

An elephant graveyard.

An ivory mausoleum.

For this bitter, vindictive man, it was the most hallowed of all places. Here his revenge was brought in, weighed and graded, recorded and stacked. Every tusk a triumph, a small piece of vengeance for a ruined life.

He looked down at his leg, as he had a million times before, then back at the tusks.

His mind reversed time. Plunged it back to that day, almost fifty years ago now, when his life had been suddenly, irreversibly changed.

He saw himself young again, muscled, hard and powerful, running with ease across Serengeti, stalking his prey. His hand came up to his beard, remembering how, in his youth, its redness had shone in the Serengeti sun. Remembered how he had been handsome and fit and joyful at life and could have run all day.

Remembered himself whole.

In his mind the moment returned, as it had interminably, every day of his life, when all had been destroyed.

A simple shoot gone wrong.

A small herd of elephant playing in the water. Noisy. Unsuspecting. Sitting targets. The satisfying thump of bullets into flesh. The excitement of their screams and bellows coursing through his blood. The sheer pleasure of the killing, the joy of the slaughter.

And then, the moment.

Out of nowhere the calf, running for its life, straight at him; the hurried re-sighting of the rifle; the missed shot; the numbing thud as he was knocked flying.

The sickening crack and crunch of splintering bone as his leg was crushed. The pain, the terrible pain, as they jolted him to Nairobi in the Land Rover, every rut and bump a white-hot branding-iron plunging into him. The days of delirium and agony. The foul stench of gangrene and the fear that they would take his leg from him. The interminable recovery and re-learning to walk.

The long, dark descent of the soul into what he had become.

Fifty years ago.

And not a day without the memory.

So here, stretched the length of this grim building, was his vengeance stacked white and high.

Here, both in fact and in symbol, a thousand elephants had repaid their debt.

But it was not enough.

Here *every* elephant would eventually repay him. Not until every elephant on earth was dead would he know peace.

Not even if he eventually found and killed the one who had done this terrible thing to him would he be sated.

Not even if he killed him, the one who had grown to such great size and become so wise and wily and dangerous that they called him Papa Tembo, *the father of elephants*, would he stop.

When they were *all* gone, then he would stop.

Sighing heavily, Laurens van der Wel closed the shed doors and limped back the way he had come.

Sher-*thunk*. Sher-*thunk*. Sher-*thunk*.

SIX

'The elephant is very difficult to live with.'

Maasai herdsman, Tanzania, 1986

Another memory. Before trust was entirely gone.

He was hungry. He was almost always hungry. The search for food was constant and debilitating and, in the terrible year of the drought, almost impossible.

That was the year the siringet, *the great Serengeti Plain, had stunk of death.*

The short rains had not come at all, so no new grass had grown. Animals had died by the million. Wildebeest, already exhausted by their migration, had failed to find food; mothers had stopped producing milk and their new-born calves had wasted away in their tens of thousands before their lives had begun. Great herds of zebra and antelope and gazelle were wiped out. Elephant wandered aimlessly, searching for food over vast distances, their presence advertised by the loud rumblings of their empty stomachs — the deepest sound of any animal on earth except the whale.

Only the carrion-eaters had done well that year, the sly

hyenas and gargoyle vultures lazily plying their putrescent trade in the glut of food around them.

He had been young and strong in that year. But even so had only just survived.

The grass of the plain did not renew itself. What there was was so short he could not scythe it with his sharp toenails, nor tear it up with his trunk. The trees withered, became leafless and died.

Every day he walked and walked.

Some days he was lucky and found a living tree. Most days what he found was already eaten bare. So he was driven further and further from the familiar places, the places of his growing, to new areas. Closer to man.

He had become used to the sight of men herding animals on the edges of his territory. They offered him no harm so he ignored them.

But now, in the year of the drought, instinct told him that where they went there would be food. Wary at first, he followed a herd at a distance, observing carefully.

No one bothered him. No one seemed even to be aware of him.

Gaining in confidence daily, he moved closer and found that he was right. The herds were being taken to food, to places the men knew. To hillsides where rainforest kept the ground moist and grass still grew.

He moved closer and began to feed with the cattle, gratefully.

And once again he was betrayed.

Feeding quietly and alone, in a thicket, he suddenly found himself surrounded by a group of red-robed men, angrily shouting, driving him off.

Confused and afraid he stood his ground briefly, but had known himself to be weakened by hunger and no match for them.

The group had closed on him, prodding at him with spears, so he had turned and run away.

And that would have been the end of it, except that, as a parting shot, one of the Maasai needlessly, petulantly, threw a spear at him. It embedded itself in his flank.

That was the memory.

The pain of the wound. The sharp, stabbing agony as he rubbed against a tree to dislodge the spear. The days of fever and throbbing anguish as the wound became infected and a deep, fly-boiling ulcer festered in his flesh. The constant, gnawing hurt as he tried to walk.

Another memory. Another hatred.

SEVEN

'We seek him here, we seek him there.'

Baroness Orczy, *The Scarlet Pimpernel*, 1905

'So, what's with this van der Wel guy? Is he a loony or what?'

Hyram was perched on the edge of the centre back seat of the Land Rover, leaning over between Benny, who was driving, and Mike in the front passenger seat. He had to shout to make himself heard over the music blasting from the car stereo.

'I see you still skirt delicately around things and take your time to get to the point,' yelled Mike. 'I thought you Americans were into political correctness now and didn't use words like "loony".'

'Huh,' snorted Hyram, wiping the sweat from his brow with his shirt sleeve. 'A loony's still a goddamn loony whatever you call him.'

Benny's face split into a wide grin. He was genuinely delighted to see this brusque, big-hearted man again.

'And anyway,' added Mike, 'it's pronounced van der *Vel*. With a "V".'

'So the guy can't spell his name either. Schmuck. What's the matter with him?'

'I don't know what's the matter with him,' Mike snapped back, irritably. 'I don't know the man.'

He glowered at the windscreen.

'For goodness' sake, Hyram, you've only been back in Tanzania ten minutes and already you've got me rattled. What with you and this blasted tape-recorder of Benny's I'll be demented by the time we get to Arusha.'

He leaned over and ejected the tape violently.

'Thanks for the fifty dollars, *bwana*,' said Benny. 'We Tanzanians can never afford such things without dollars.'

''Course you can't,' Hyram replied. 'Not on what this schmuck pays you. Turn it back on if he's got nothing useful to say.'

'I said I didn't know him,' snorted Mike. 'I didn't say I didn't know *about* him. First things first. How about taking a chisel to your wallet. Petrol's five dollars a gallon on the black market. We've already spent your two hundred dollars. And we've still to discuss the money I've lost from turning parties of tourists away so I can take you on your crazy jaunt.'

Benny coughed loudly and choked. The last tourists had been months ago and he knew full well that none was booked.

'*Bwana*,' he said, reproachfully.

'Nah, don't worry, Benny. I know the guy's lying.' Hyram grinned widely, enjoying the joke. 'Money ain't no problem to me. I got other problems.'

'Yes, your weight's one, your mouth's another. Neither's improved since you were last here,' said Mike, acidly.

'Yeah, quite true, happily,' Hyram agreed. 'But I got a bigger problem. Conscience. That's why I'm here.'

'I know,' said Mike quietly. 'I know.'

'I ain't been the same, I can tell you, since we saw them goddamn Somalis hacking at them poor goddamn elephants' heads all those years ago.'

There was a silence as the three men's minds instantly returned to the day, five years ago, when, driving on remote Maasai herding tracks between Lake Natron and the Kenyan border, they had come upon the horrific sight of poachers in the very act of chopping out the tusks from the skulls of three recently slaughtered elephants.

Hyram, the innocent, unsuspecting tourist had been profoundly shocked and distressed. Mike, ex-game warden, disillusioned cynic, witness to a thousand senseless violences perpetrated on animals, had been enraged to the point of murder. For there is, more than with any other animal, a deep, primeval bond between elephant and man. Somehow, the elephant's extended childhood, his great size, his long life, his amiable, massive quietness touch an ancient, recognizable chord. He has no enemies in all the animal world. His strength is immense, prehistoric. His brain can reason. He can be fearsome, gentle, devious and loving. He can sing and dance. He can sorrow and grieve and cry.

Of all the animals on earth he can be the most awesome, the most deadly, the most dangerous.

And yet, strangely, he seems so vulnerable, so capable of being harmed. His vast strength is rarely used in anger. His fearsome snortings and stampings and charges are nearly always sham.

A gentle, baggy-trousered giant.

But one who carries a great and tragic curse. A curse that has brought his race to the precipice of extinction.

The beauty of his tusks dooms him. Dooms him to be harried and driven, pierced with arrows and spears, torn apart with bullets.

For what?

For Arabs to pose grandly, ivory-handled daggers at their waists. For simpering women with dead-white necklaces and bracelets to set off their golden tans. For ornaments. For door handles. For piano keys. For rings and brooches and buttons. For billiard balls.

For these trivial things a great, majestic, unique life ends.

'No sir,' snarled Hyram, as he contemplated for the thousandth time the picture burned deep in his mind. 'I ain't been the same and I won't ever be. Sometimes I go and wander around Times Square and look at all the weirdos and psychos and loonies and then I think of Serengeti and these big, grey Dumbos just wandering about happy and harming goddamn no one, and I says to myself, "Who's the better goddamn race? Who's the *nice* fellas?" And then some goddamn jerk comes along and goddamn shoots them and they end up with their goddamn teeth on some goddamn fancypants goddamn mantelpiece. It makes me goddamn ill.'

'Has anyone ever pointed out to you that you have what may be termed a colourful turn of phrase?' asked Mike, mildly.

'Too right they have. And what's more it's bothered

me all these years that we never caught up with those Somali poachers. I still blame you for that. Goddamn Great White Hunters are supposed to know how to track people.'

'I told you then and I'll tell you now,' said Mike. 'My hunting, tracking days are long over. They finished when I left Selous Reserve. I'm not a game warden any longer. I'm a tour guide. I take awkward cusses like you to nice safe water-holes to snap hippos having baths. Poachers aren't my business. Though sometimes they might be easier to handle than what I get. I don't know what sins I ever committed to get *you*.'

'Pull the other one. I was behind you that day, remember? You were a tour guide then too. A tour guide with a semi-automatic rifle. I saw you shooting at those guys. You weren't playing games. You were shooting to kill.'

'Maybe,' said Mike. 'Maybe.'

There was a short silence.

'Anyway, let's start again, shall we?' said Hyram eventually. 'What's with this van der Wel guy? Is he a loony or what?'

Mike groaned under his breath. When Hyram wanted something, Hyram persisted.

'He's shadowy. No one seems to know the man personally, though that doesn't stop people sounding off about him. He doesn't seem the type to win popularity contests. He has an office in Moshi, with a warehouse behind. "Toma Import and Export", he calls himself. But it's run by an African manager. Van der Wel never shows up.'

'Importing and exporting what, as if I didn't know?' said Hyram. 'Have you taken a look?'

'No. No point. He couldn't get away with anything there – it's too open. That place is straightforward – coffee, sugar, tea – that sort of thing. It's next door to the police station.'

'Oh yeah, police. Big difference that's going to make.'

'It's a front, Hyram, a front. It gives him an office. It gives him a legitimate phone number where business transactions can take place, OK? He can't have a phone wherever he hides out, so messages presumably get relayed to him by his stooges. Didn't you ever read any crime novels?'

'Right. So where's his real operation? And yes, professor, I did read a book once but it hurt my goddamn head so I didn't try another.'

'Hyram, you get me down. What do you think we all are here? Fools? If anybody knew where his real operation was, or even *what* it was, don't you think we'd be doing something about it? You might not have a very high opinion of the police at the moment, but they're not all dishonest here. If they could prove anything they'd pick him up. The man's clever. We hear rumours. But rumour is all there's ever been. Nobody's ever got near to proving he's poaching. That's what I mean by shadowy. He flits here and there. When the light changes, he's gone.'

'So, big deal. The Scarlet goddamn Pimpernel. So tell me, are elephant tusks shadows? Do they goddamn flit about? Elephant tusks is big. Elephant tusks is very heavy. You don't walk about with elephant tusks in your goddamn pockets without somebody noticing.'

'Hyram, you've forgotten. This is Africa. You've forgotten the size. I could take this Land Rover out on to the other side of Arusha, point you north-west on to Serengeti and you could drive a thousand kilometres in a straight line and never see a village, never see another vehicle, never see a human being. Except, of course, you'd drive straight into Lake Victoria and drown, which is the best thought I've had today.'

'Jeez, I never met a man like you. You're such a goddamn defeatist.'

Hyram slumped back into his seat again.

'Realist, Hyram,' Mike snapped. '*Realist*. If a man wants to vanish in Africa, he can. If van der Wel wants to kill elephants he'll know just where to do it out of sight of anyone. If any locals see him he'll buy them off with the meat. An elephant will feed a whole village for a month; they're not going to complain. They don't see animals in the same light as we do anyway. They're there to eat. And as for the tusks, nothing could be easier. Loaded into the back of a Bedford MK truck they can be taken anywhere overnight with ease. Bedfords don't need roads, they'll cross any sort of country. Van der Wel can cross borders into Rwanda, Uganda or Kenya at any one of a thousand places.'

'Dee-fee-tist!' snorted Hyram. 'These trucks, they drive undergoddamnground, I suppose? They drive silent, I suppose? They don't leave tracks, I suppose? Some trucks. Ingoddamnvisible. The US Army might be interested in them.'

He went silent for a while, brooding darkly and glaring out of the Land Rover window.

Eventually he brightened.

'Benny?' he said.

'Yes, *bwana*.'

'I'm going to talk to you instead. This guy's giving

51

me anxiety. What do the Africans say? Do they know this van der Wel?'

'Well, *bwana* . . .' Benny replied.

'Be careful,' warned Mike. 'Give this man an inch and he'll have us careering about the country for a month on a wild-goose chase.'

'Well,' said Benny, 'I have this friend, Maasai man, whose friend has a cousin who lives . . .'

Mike Taylor sighed wearily, slid down in his seat and closed his eyes.

' . . . out near Ol Doinyo Lengai, who says . . .'

'Wonderful,' exclaimed Hyram, joyfully. He slapped Benny so hard on the back that the Land Rover veered out into the middle of the road. There was a great screeching of tyres as Benny fought the big machine back into a straight line again.

'Wonderful. Now we're getting somewhere. Tomorrow we'll go see him. You hear that, Taylor?'

Mike Taylor didn't reply.

'Taylor, you hear? You want me to open my wallet, right? So, tomorrow I will. We're off to see this old Don Yolen guy, OK?'

Mike Taylor winced silently and pretended to be asleep.

EIGHT

'We had seen instantaneously coordinated behaviour of a group of elephants which made us think that one animal had given an alarm call that we could not hear.'

Cynthia Moss, *Elephant Memories*, 1988

7.30 a.m. Herd spread out. 5/2, 5/5, 5/7, feeding at edge of swamp on Cynodon dactylon. *5/1, 5/3, 5/4, 5/6, feeding on* Acacia xanthophloea. *5/9, 5/11, drinking. 5/12, Mud Bath. 5/10 absent. 5/8 standing guard.*

Alison Blake looked over her father's shoulder at what he was recording in the diary.

'What's *Cynodon dactylon?*' she enquired.

'Grass.'

'Oh, how interesting.'

'Don't be sarcastic. It's important information.'

'Yes, I'm sure it is.'

'Half the point of this study,' said John Blake impatiently, 'is that this area is becoming overgrazed by Maasai cattle. You've seen the Maasai herds. Some-

53

times one herd is a thousand animals now. In the not too distant future we may have to help these elephants move, otherwise they're going to get very hungry indeed.'

'Hm,' said Alison, not convinced that the elephants couldn't manage to seek out new food for themselves.

She wandered over to where Matt was sitting at the edge of a small bluff overlooking the herd.

'Where's Cleopatra?' she asked.

'She's there, just at the edge of the water, throwing mud on herself,' Matt replied.

The elephant was curving her trunk, scooping up the dark, glutinous substance and throwing it onto her back with a sound like the sharp thwack of flapping wet sheets. She was rapidly turning from grey to black.

'Messy business,' said Matt, 'but the sun's starting to get hot already. She knows she needs the protection.'

Alison sat down beside him.

'I hope she hangs on a couple of days. It would be nice if she calved on my birthday. A perfect present.'

'It's the only present you're likely to get out here,' her brother responded.

'I've forgotten who some of the adults are now, though I recognize all the calves, I think. Ten months is a long time.'

'Mmm. Miserable was it, school?'

'Isn't it always? I spent most of the time looking out of the window and seeing this place in my mind. And England's so cold and wet.'

'Glad to be back then, are you?'

'Are you kidding? I couldn't wait. Anyway, I don't want to talk about school. Or even think about it for the next two months. I've just about had enough. I don't know whether I can stand going back for A levels.'

'I know. I couldn't wait to get out either. I suppose some time I'll have to do the conventional thing and go to university, but I'll put it off as long as I can. Every day I thank my lucky stars that Dad wangled me this job as his assistant. I hope the study lasts for ever.'

'It's been going since I was a baby. There's no reason why it shouldn't continue, so long as the government keeps up the money. Have you got the Ear Book?'

'It's in the bag there, beside you.'

Alison delved into the leather bag and produced a small blue notebook. She flicked through the pages. Their system of identification was simple. Each page bore an individual elephant's number and a drawing of its ear. Ears are elephant's fingerprints; their shape changes hardly at all from birth to death.

Alison moved her eyes from picture to herd and back again, reminding herself of the ones she had forgotten.

Some needed no reminder and were quickly identified just by their great age and size. An elephant grows all its life. The bigger the elephant the older it is, so the huge bulks of the ancient matriarch Queen Victoria, bad tempered and never amused, and her fussy, solicitous sister, Aunt Emily, stood out from the rest. At the moment Queen Victoria was happily munching a thorn bush while Emily was lurking close to the pregnant Cleopatra, hoping her help would soon be needed.

In the Ear Book they were recorded as '5/1 (f) age 65–70', and '5/2 (f) age 60–65'.

Alison snorted.

'That's what I mean about numbers,' she grumbled. 'They tell you nothing.'

The middle-sized cows were the ones she had forgotten, but gradually she sorted them all out again into their family groups. Queen Victoria's three female children, Gertrude, Ann and the flirt Jezebel, were all still in calving age.

Alison searched around the herd until she found Gertrude. She and her sons, Hamlet and Horatio, were feeding on grasses and sedges.

'Hamlet will be getting ready to leave soon, won't he? How old is he now?'

'He's ten, so in theory he'll go off on his own sometime in the next year. But only in theory. He's a great, soft baby. I guess he'll cling on to his mother's apron strings until he's about twenty.'

Alison grinned. They'd named the calf Hamlet because he looked so tragic and forlorn and lost all the time.

'Dorothy's son, Daffodil, will go first,' Matt continued. 'He's been showing signs for some months. He wanders off all the time now by himself. Sometimes he comes back at night, sometimes he stays away. Dorothy's fed up with him. She never seems pleased to see him when he turns up. He goes and stands near Aunt Emily for comfort. She looks after everyone.'

'She's his grandmother, so of course she'll look after him. Is he here now?'

'No. He disappeared a couple of days ago. When the herd stopped he kept on walking. Just ignored the others and loped on as though he had somewhere he had to go.'

Alison smiled and gazed affectionately at the herd.

'Funny, isn't it? They're so strange. And yet so much like us.'

'They're the only land mammal with a brain larger than man's. That must tell us something,' Matt said.

'Hm.' Alison pondered the thought. 'Interesting. Though it wouldn't take much to have a larger brain than the men in my family. Come on. Time for breakfast.'

She jumped to her feet before her brother could hit her, and ran back to the Land Rover.

The elephants fed and drank without pause until noon, moving now and then from one type of food to another. John and Matt Blake studiously recorded the names of the numerous grasses and sedges, bushes and herbs that they favoured.

Alison was more interested in their individual quirks. Boxer, Jezebel's eight-year-old son, was in an annoying mood, periodically breaking off from his feeding to chase madly around in high spirits and spar with the other male calves. Horatio, a little older and more dignified, eventually grew tired of this importunate nuisance and charged Boxer, knocking him over onto his side. Boxer retreated, subdued for a while, but soon recovered and went to annoy the young female calf, Elizabeth, who was much smaller than he and easier prey. Eventually Jezebel gave her errant son a sound whack with her trunk and sent him off sulking under a tree. Alison grinned at the similarity with human families.

Eventually the herd began to lose interest in feeding and started to move out from the swamp onto slightly higher ground where they found a patch of dusty soil. The adults scooped the dust up with the tips of their trunks and sprayed it over their heads and backs. The youngest of the calves, still not adept at this, were helped by the adults, with Aunt Emily spraying the young Elizabeth.

That done, the herd settled to rest in a tight group. The calves, one by one, sank down and rolled over onto their sides. Grunting and rumbling, the adults slowly shuffled themselves into a circle around them, pushing the pregnant Cleopatra into the middle also. Gradually their heads began to hang down. Some draped their trunks over their tusks, others let them hang limply down, their tips touching the ground. The rumbling and shuffling gradually ceased and all became quiet.

They slept for about an hour, the calves dead to the world, but the adults watchful even in sleep. Now and then an eye would flick open, an alert ear would flap suspiciously or a trunk raise slightly to sniff the air.

The humans rested too. There was nothing to record, nothing to watch. John Blake slept. Matt and Alison sat with their backs against trees, enjoying the silence and space. Far in the distance a herd of zebra moved across the plain, heat melting them into a shimmering mirage.

And then – *something*.

Simultaneously, as though on a given order, the adult elephants were all awake and alert again. At precisely the same instant every eye opened, every head lifted and turned.

'Matt, look,' Alison whispered.

'I know. I saw it.' He got to his feet, looking around anxiously.

'What is it?'

'I don't know. Perhaps they've picked up the scent of a lion or something. I can't see anything. Go wake Dad, will you?'

'Right.' Alison jumped up and ran back up the slope to her father.

The elephant group started to break up. The matriarch, Queen Victoria, gave a deep rumble then stamped quickly away from the others, her head high, her great ears flapping. The mothers rapidly nudged their sleeping calves onto their feet, prodding them urgently with their tusks until they were fully awake. Then they all fell quickly into line behind their leader.

Within a few short seconds the whole herd was on the move, the adults loping with a loose, floppy gait, the calves trotting at their sides, struggling to keep up.

'Strange,' said John Blake when he appeared at his son's side. 'Can you see anything?'

Matt was scanning round with the binoculars.

'Nothing. There's a few gazelle and wildebeest wandering about down there and they're not disturbed at all. Mysterious. I've never seen them take off quite like that before.'

'I know. And they're going at quite a lick. Come on, let's get after them and see what's going on.'

'I hope Cleopatra's all right,' Alison said, beginning to gather up the notebooks and stuff them back in the bag. 'She shouldn't be dashing about like that in her condition.'

Hurriedly they scrambled into the Land Rover and bounced away in pursuit.

NINE

'The elephant is the only terrestrial mammal to communicate using infrasound — sound below the range of human hearing. Some of the sounds recorded have been at pressure levels of 115 decibels. Such a sound could easily travel up to six miles.'

Warden of Tarangire National Park, Tanzania, speaking to the author, 1986

He stood quietly under a spreading thorn tree waiting for dawn. It would not, his senses told him, be long in coming.

The weaver birds stirred and argued irritably in their secure nests above his head and fireflies danced, like a million stars, through the branches, enjoying their last flickers of luminous white light before the rising sun extinguished them. The whole tree sparked and hummed with life, all of it unconcerned by his presence below.

He could smell the sun lying just below the

horizon. The smell of night mists swirling away to daytime hiding places.

Hunger was gnawing at him, urging him to move, to start the long daily battle for food. He tried to ignore it, to ignore the deep rumblings of complaint from his stomach. He needed to wait until the warmth of the sun touched his skin, sank into him and eased the aches in his back and legs. The night had been very cold. Cold enough to penetrate him and chill his bones.

He had slept fitfully. In the small hours the faint cough of a lion had clicked his eyes open, but it was far off and he had little fear of lions anyway.

Later a leopard had floated by, walking on air, silent as a grave, but heard nevertheless. He ignored that too. Few things, he knew, would approach him; fewer still would attempt to do him harm.

The night had passed and the new day was beginning.

The plain was lightening gradually now. The dark mushroom shapes dotted, hunched and black around him were resolving themselves into trees as the first greys of dawn-light turned to silver. A soft, golden glow drew a long brush-stroke on the horizon and he felt the first, gentle warmth of the day begin to suffuse his skin. Slowly the pale crescent of the emerging sun slid up past the far edge of the world and bathed his whole body.

Grunting a little with pleasure he began to move his legs, lifting each foot up from the grass and returning it, easing his stiffened knees. Eventually he began to walk out from under the tree, slowly and limpingly at first.

The birds harangued him noisily, but it was only a show, a pretence of alarm. Emerging from their nests they fluttered and chattered around his head. Then, their token protest registered, they returned, complaining, to their nests.

He ignored them and headed out on to open ground. In the far distance a long, black line of wildebeest divided land from sky. They paused momentarily, their instinct noting his presence, then, deciding that he offered no threat, resumed their strange, endless journey to nowhere.

So began another day, walking in search of food.

He had no direction. Here, on the vastness of the plains, any direction was as good as any other. Whichever way he went he would eventually find food and water.

He walked. And gradually the walking became easier. Soon, warmed by the building heat of the sun and by his movement, he fell into a steady, plodding rhythm which would, if necessary, carry him effortlessly for huge distances. As he walked he constantly scanned the plain, taking in the herds of grazing zebra, the gazelles and the countless thousands of wildebeest moving like great, dark clouds across the grass. Away in the distance his keen ears caught the vile croak of vultures squabbling wildly over carrion. He snorted gently with revulsion at the thought of them.

Then he identified a large baobab tree in the distance and turned towards it. Baobab meant succulent, delicious food. His mouth began to salivate in anticipation and his stomach rumbled harder.

And then suddenly, without any warning, the day changed.

This day, which had started out like any other, became a different day. A day long ago. A day far back in his life but ever-present in the dark and private corners of his mind.

In the distance, so faint that it was barely heard, came a low, protracted lament of animal pain.

He swung his head round and listened.

The cry was repeated.

The drawn-out, profoundly distressed howl of a trapped and injured elephant whispered across the great distances of the plains and settled, reverberating disquietingly, in his ears.

Instantly he was transformed, as though a switch had been clicked on in his placid brain. A searing, white-hot surge of rage tore through him.

A cry like that was alien. It was not a cry of anger or challenge or warning. No natural threat or danger would produce a sound of such bafflement and fear, mingled with the pain.

Such distress meant only one thing.

Man, the greatest enemy, was involved.

He stopped momentarily as he was transported back through time, back almost to the beginning of his life. To another day that had started out in calm and safety, but had been torn apart with cries like this.

Now, half a century later, the picture scorched through his mind, etched in colours as vivid as the day that it had happened.

He saw again the redness of the blood. The grotesque dance of the wounded and the terrible stillness of the dead.

Heard again the screams of pain.

Maddened by the memory he began to sway from side to side, his great head swinging on an axis of rage.

He began to stamp the ground, lifting his feet and thudding them down again, all his massive weight pounding the earth in deep drumbeats which pulsed away across the plains.

He lifted his head and bellowed once. A thunderclap of sound welled up from deep in his body.

A great, primeval cry rattled out across the plains. 'I hear you,' his cry said. *'I hear you.'*

And a million creatures felt the rumble of the earth, a million heads lifted, wonderingly, at the sound.

He turned, pinpointed the direction from which the anguished cry had come and, food now forgotten, set off with a long, determined lope across the plain.

TEN

*'In this country everything is impossible. Unless
you have money.'*

East-African newspaper reporter, speaking to the
author, 1986

They turned off the main Arusha-Nairobi road at the
dilapidated, crossroads village of Makayune and headed
north. A couple of kilometres further on, the tarmac
ran out and the road became dirt. Here Benny pulled
into a garage where he had an 'arrangement' about
petroli.

'Garage' was perhaps too grand a word for a rusted,
corrugated-iron shed and a single, medieval, hand-
cranked petrol pump with a sign saying 'CLOSED'
hung on it.

'It's closed,' observed Hyram, reasonably.

'Hyram,' replied Mike, 'shut up. Leave it to
Benny. Every petrol pump in the country has "closed"
on it. It doesn't mean it *is* closed. This is Africa.'

'Right,' said Hyram.

'The owner here is a Chagga,' said Benny, as he slid out of the driving seat. 'My tribe.'

'Ah,' said Hyram.

'But I'll need the money now even so, *bwana*,' Benny continued. 'No money to show, no talk.'

'Yeah, of course. Here, then.'

Hyram dug into his back pocket and pulled out a wad of sweat-stained fifty-dollar bills.

'That enough?'

'We'll see,' replied Mike. 'There's been no petrol in Tanzania for five months. The government doesn't have the hard currency to buy any, so they say, and the Tanzanian shilling won't buy anything. They have to sell coffee or sugar abroad to get the dollars to buy petrol. But, of course, "no petrol" doesn't mean there's no petrol. This is—'

'Yeah, yeah, I know,' Hyram interrupted. 'This is Africa.'

A very ragged, sleep-numbed man emerged from the depths of the shed, scratching his stomach.

Benny took him briskly by the arm and marched him round behind the shed. It was several minutes before they reappeared, but when they did Benny was wearing a victorious grin.

Looking furtively up and down the road the Chagga fumbled in his pocket, produced a large key and unlocked the big padlock on the petrol pump. He placed the nozzle into the Land Rover's tank and began to wind the crank-handle laboriously. The pump wheezed and screeched, but above that the satisfying sound of gurgling liquid could be heard.

The Land Rover had three tanks, all interconnected, each holding a hundred litres, so the filling was still going on half an hour later.

'Jeez,' muttered an incredulous Hyram. 'In New York they'd shoot this guy.'

'We've a long way to go yet,' Mike replied, pointing to the rows of dark-green, metal jerrycans chained to the roof-rack.

'Another two hundred and fifty litres up there. If he's got that much.'

Benny climbed up onto the roof-rack and snapped open the caps of the cans in readiness. When the main, built-in tanks were finally full the nozzle was passed up to him, the Chagga continued cranking and gradually, very gradually, Benny moved along the rows filling each can.

'Jeez,' said Hyram, periodically – stunned by the building heat of the morning and the funereal pace of the task.

'Patience, Hyram,' Mike advised. 'This is—'

'Don't say it,' snarled Hyram, through clenched teeth. 'Just don't say it.'

An hour and five minutes and $650 later, they were ready to move on.

'*How much?*' Hyram yelled, when Benny told him.

'Six hundred and fifty dollars, *bwana*. Five hundred and fifty litres at a dollar a litre, plus the hundred dollars I had to give him to open the pump at all – six hundred and fifty dollars. Sorry *bwana*, it's the way things are here.'

'Jeez, I wish I'd stayed in jail.'

'So do we,' said Mike, grinning. 'But you wanted *petroli* – now you've got it. And aren't you the man who only yesterday said, "Money ain't no problem to me"?'

'OK, OK. You did good, Benny. How far will we get on this?'

'Depends on what we do,' Mike answered. 'This is a big, thirsty beast at the best of times. Unladen, on a good, metalled road, six kilometres to the litre. Weighed down like this, three. If we do a lot of rough, cross-country stuff, with four-wheel-drive and low ratio, perhaps only one. Say an average of three and we've got about sixteen hundred kilometres. In Africa that's not as much as it sounds. All depends on where we have to go.'

'So, let's go *somewhere* then. Let's get on the goddamn move. The way we've started we'll all be dead of old age before we see an elephant.'

'You're the boss,' said Mike, saluting in his tour operator mode.

'At six hundred and fifty dollars, too goddamn right I am.'

The journey was long, arduous and very dusty. With each kilometre that passed, the track became more neglected and less discernible until, by the time they reached the Ol Kerii Escarpment, it had vanished altogether.

Here the plain was cut through with deep gullies carved into the soft earth by the torrents of water pouring off the steep sides of the Ngorongoro Crater during the wet season. Progress became desperately slow as time and again they would find their path blocked by sheer-sided chasms, sometimes as much as ten metres deep. Grumbling quietly to himself Benny would drive slowly along the side of a gully until he found a negotiable crossing.

'Negotiable', in Benny's book, did not always mean the same thing to Mike.

'Dear God,' he would shout as the Land Rover tilted almost vertically down a slope and slid, uncontolled, into a gully bottom.

'What do you think you're doing, Benny? We'll never get out of this.'

But Benny would just grin his long-suffering grin, heave the red-topped lever into low-ratio and grind the big machine slowly up the other side of the gully. Mike and Hyram would be thrown violently backwards and forwards as the vehicle's wheels spun in the fine volcanic dust.

'At least it's a bit of excitement,' said Hyram. 'I never seen such boring country. I ain't seen an animal since Makayune, and that was only a dog.'

'Nothing comes out here much,' Mike replied. 'It's a swamp in the wet, a huge heat-trap in the dry. Even the wildebeest skirt around this. They go south of Ngorongoro or north of Lake Natron on their migration. Anything you see out here's lost.'

'And that's another thing I've been meaning to ask. I ain't seen no track for hours. You guys sure you know where you are?'

Mike snorted with annoyance.

'You may have noticed a small hill to our left, which we've been passing all morning – though, given that it's only about four thousand metres high and about thirty kilometres long, you could be forgiven for missing it. That's Ngorongoro Crater. Ol Doinyo Lengai is just to the north of it. Unless someone's moved Ngorongoro it's going to be very difficult to get lost.'

'You lost them poachers that time. I ain't trusted you since.'

Benny chortled softly to himself. Mike glared a warning at him and they continued in silence.

ELEVEN

'Ol Kerii . . . that part of the Rift Escarpment that stands opposite a remote volcano known to the Maasai as ol doinyo le eng ai, *the Mountain of God.'*

East-African guidebook

To go to Ol Doinyo Lengai is to take a journey not just in distance, but in time.

The other great volcanic peaks of Meru and Kilimanjaro, after aeons of fire and violence, are at peace. Their slopes are thickly covered with cool rainforest, alive with the colour and song of bright birds and rattling to the comic chatter of monkeys. Leopards prowl, invisible and soundless, in the great, dark folds of their valleys, and water buffalo, clumsy and foultempered, lumber from waterhole to waterhole, arguing with braying hippos. Elephants stand under trees, quiet as rocks, their grey bulks mere pools of shadow, or, like living bulldozers, grind slowly through the forest destroying everything in their paths. Stand and listen and you will hear the great trees crack and fall. Stand and listen and you know the mountains live.

Ol Doinyo Lengai is different. She has not surrendered, not given up her hold on time.

Stand at Ol Doinyo Lengai and you stand at that strange pause, millennia ago, when the earth began to cool and the spittings of molten earth began to die away. When titanic fires had faded to embers and were laying carpets of fine ash upon the earth. When running lava crusted into valleys, and clouds of steam resolved into lakes.

At that finely balanced moment when the world held its breath and waited for life to begin.

Ol Doinyo Lengai still waits. In all the millennia, life has not come to her slopes.

Nor does she want it. She throws out fire still, still belches angry steam. Her flanks smoulder yet, so no feet ascend her, no seed can find a lodging, no root a place of purchase.

Sulphur hangs in the air, foul and tactile, all around her, and sinks down into the very waters of the lakes and streams.

A silent, arid, lifeless place.

Lonely as the moon.

A perfect place to hide.

TWELVE

'The Maasai, men of cattle, always seeking grass and water, live in small scattered clusters here and there, like momentary parts of a landscape.'

Iain and Oria Douglas-Hamilton,
Among the Elephants, 1975

It was late afternoon when they finally arrived at the Maasai *manyatta*.

At first they thought it deserted. The thorn-tree branches which served as a gate were pulled aside, so they drove straight in and stopped in the central clearing. A circle of windowless huts surrounded them, their walls dark and rough from plastered cattle dung, their roofs neatly thatched.

Benny switched off the engine.

The village appeared lifeless, the only sound a constant, background hum of flies, the only movement some emaciated, lethargic hens scratching at the dust and mindlessly pecking at nothing on the ground.

They waited.

Hyram wrinkled his nose in distaste.

'Jeez,' he remarked mildly, sniffing the air.

A heavy, acrid odour seeped in through the Land Rover windows. The stench of dung and urine and sour milk and dried blood which hangs over every Maasai village.

Hyram pulled out a handkerchief and held it over his nose.

Mike smiled, enjoying his discomfort.

'You'll get used to it,' he said. 'They live without water most of the time. These plains don't hold much water. The cattle can usually get enough moisture from the grasses — but now and then the Maasai will herd them out to distant waterholes. The people do without. They drink milk from the cattle but hardly ever eat meat. They drain blood from the animals' legs, mix it with some milk and leave it a few days. It turns into a sort of semi-solid yoghurt. I'm told it's quite tasty.'

'Jeez,' said Hyram again. He had turned slightly pale.

'And then,' Mike continued, warming to his subject, 'they wash out their gourds with urine before putting fresh milk in them, and also . . .'

'All right, all right, I get the picture. I can do without all the details.'

'Just thought you'd like to know,' said Mike, happily.

They waited in silence, Hyram breathing heavily behind his handkerchief.

Eventually, curiosity overcoming their nervousness, a few heads began to poke from dark doorways and figures began to emerge. Old women sidled out and stood in the shadows of huts, grinning toothlessly. Young women, with babies at their hips, stepped out with more confidence, and small children congregated in protective groups, giggling and hiding their faces behind over-large hands.

'All the able-bodied men will be out with the cattle,' said Benny, as they climbed out of the Land Rover. 'They won't be far away.'

Hyram looked out beyond the fence and turned slowly in a complete circle. In every direction the plains stretched away into infinity, empty and featureless.

'Huh,' he said. 'Not far away, eh? You got eyes? There's nothing out there.'

He swiped irritably at the flies circling around his head.

'Leave the flies alone!' ordered Mike. 'Flies are ancestors in Maasai tradition. It's an affront to brush them away. If you upset these people we'll learn nothing.'

'And look out there again,' added Benny, pointing to the north. 'They're there.'

Hyram screwed up his eyes against the glare and stared hard in the direction Benny indicated.

Far, far out, where land and cloud merged on the horizon, a faint, diffuse, red smudge shimmered and shifted in the heat-laden distance.

'That's their dust cloud. They're on their way back. They'll be here by dusk. Until then we just wait.'

Hyram reached through the Land Rover window and pulled out Mike's powerful binoculars. Grunting with the effort, he climbed up on to the bonnet of the Land Rover and planted his feet firmly on the spare wheel. Then he trained the binoculars on the red cloud and turned the focusing wheel.

'Yeah, you're right,' he said, as the picture became clear. I see them.'

Then he fell silent.

The scene itself silenced him, for, strangely, binoculars do not *reveal* a scene, they *create* it. They take the user out of reality and supplant him elsewhere. Reality is immediacy – what you see, here and now, with your eyes; what is close; what you can touch.

Viewed through a magical lens, reality, time and distance are suspended.

Here, through glass, a scene of biblical antiquity was taking place.

A vast red dust cloud whispered slowly across the plain as the herd moved in unison towards him. Through the dust, Hyram could discern only vague shapes and colours, blotches of white and brown and black, as individual animals were momentarily illumined by shafts of sunlight and were immediately swallowed up in smoky redness. Great curved horns would swing into view, etched blackly against the red, and vanish as quickly as they came.

And, on the edges of this ghostly sea of cattle, more unreal than they, the Maasai herdsmen floated, tall and ochred – graceful outriders drifting in and out of the concealing dust; scarlet, elongated phantoms, flashing light from their burnished spears.

Hyram gasped at this eerily silent spectacle.

Cattle and dust. Heat and redness. Maasai. A moving, living distillation of Africa.

And then, as he watched, the picture began to change, to break up, before his eyes.

Cattle lifted their heads in alarm and opened their mouths wide in silent bellows of warning. The tight formation began to crumble as groups of animals broke away and started to run, panicky and directionless, away from the herd.

The Maasai herdsmen too began to run, this way and that, vainly trying to stop the madly charging animals, now appearing, now vanishing in the swirling dust. Brief, red lightning flashes in a storm of cattle.

'What the devil . . . ?' Hyram muttered to himself.

He scanned the binoculars back and forth, trying to find what was causing the panic, but could see nothing.

The confusion increased, animals thundering away in all directions, until the herd had dispersed completely. The Maasai were left waving their spears after them in a display of angry futility.

'What is it?' asked Mike. 'What's going on?'

'I don't know. Something. Wait!'

Hyram pulled the binoculars back on to the Maasai.

They had come together now, unsure and seemingly confused themselves, looking this way and that, pacing uncertainly in one direction then the other, their tall, vivid silhouettes clear against the dust cloud behind them.

Briefly they stopped and stood, stock-still, listening. Then, as one, they erupted into movement, flailing away in mad, panicked flight. Within a second they had shot out of Hyram's vision.

'Jeez,' he said again. 'What *is* this?'

The binoculars were still focused on the space the Maasai had occupied. Now there was only the heavy red curtain of the dust cloud.

And in it – *something moving*.

Something dark, of huge bulk, its shape shifting, distorted.

Hyram drew in his breath sharply with shock as the shape clarified.

The silence of distance, the strange, unearthly redness, gave the scene a nightmare, hellish unreality as the great, grey head emerged out of the red dust and into his vision. So immediate, so massive was its presence, framed in the glass of the binoculars, that instinct made him forget momentarily that distance separated them, and a sharp jolt of fear shot through him.

The elephant was moving at great speed, seeming to Hyram to emerge from fire and smoke, its trunk high, its mouth open in a bellow of anger, its ears flapping violently.

Briefly, it changed direction – once, twice – as it selected from the running Maasai, then, its decision made, fixed its eyes on the slowest moving of them and thundered after him.

Hyram watched, in terrible fascination, as the gap between pursuer and pursued rapidly closed.

He almost thought he could hear the man's terrified scream as the elephant's feet thudded, inexorably closer, in the earth behind him, and his final cry as the great, incomprehensibly powerful trunk wound around his waist and swung him effortlessly into the air.

Hyram lowered the binoculars.

'Taylor?' he said, quietly.

'What?'

'I think we'd better get on out there. Something's happened. I'll tell you what on the way.'

THIRTEEN

*'These wild animals were wiser than the men
intent on replacing them by domestic flocks and
herds, for they never overstrained the land's
capacity to feed them, as cattle did; they never
trod down the grasses and churned the ground to
pulp and scarred the earth with gullies where they
filed to water.'*

Elspeth Huxley, *The Mottled Lizard*, 1962

Benny stopped the Land Rover a few metres away from
the group of Maasai, who stood in a circle around the
man on the ground. Even from a distance the grotesque
angles of the man's limbs had made it obvious that he
was dead.

The dust had begun to settle. The cattle were
scattered across the plain. In the way all animals have
of dismissing danger as soon as it has passed, they had
resumed their grazing as though nothing had happened.

Benny switched off the engine and they sat in
silence.

'What do we do?' asked Hyram eventually.

'Nothing. Leave them to it. When they're ready we'll help them round up their cattle again and get them back to the *manyatta*. Apart from that there's nothing we *can* do.'

They watched as the men began to arrange the body.

The Maasai are not given to emotion or ceremony over death. Death is just another episode in a long journey, a journey of which the years spent on earth are only a tiny part. For the Maasai, life is present before a person is born and continues after he dies. Like the ancient symbol of a snake swallowing its tail, things have no beginning and no end.

So, there was no question of taking the dead man back to the village. They simply arranged him where he was. They laid him on his left side, knees drawn up, head to the north. His right arm they laid across his chest; his left arm they crooked under his head, cushioning it.

Then they turned his face towards the east, towards the rising sun.

'*Aia,*' the Maasai said.

And they left him.

Come the setting of the sun, the hyenas would deal with his body. When the new sun rose in the east his spirit would be elsewhere on its journey.

'Is that it?' asked Hyram. 'Is that all there is?'

'Yup,' said Mike. 'That's it.'

Without even acknowledging the presence of the visitors, the Maasai, their faces showing no emotion, turned away and headed out towards their cattle.

Things happen.

Things continue.

'*Aia.*' So be it.

'Elephant. They are vermin.'

The Maasai headman, Kibasa, spoke contemptuously and angrily.

Mike nudged Hyram, signalling him not to argue. They were seated, with all the men of the *manyatta*, in a circle at the centre of the compound, around a large, crackling fire.

'Vermin. They trample the crops in our *shambas* and smash our fences. They drink dry our waterholes so our cattle perish. They destroy our trees so we have no shade.'

The tribesmen nodded and grunted in agreement.

'And this one, Papa Tembo, he is our curse.' Kibasa spat violently into the fire to emphasize his words.

'Papa Tembo.' Mike nodded. 'I have heard tell of him, but never seen him. I have heard that the Maasai say he cannot be killed.'

'It is true. We have tried many, many times. We have dug pits but he walks around them. We have poisoned waterholes we know he uses, but he sniffs them and walks away. We have lain in wait for days with our poisoned arrows, but somehow he always knows where we are and does not come. Even the *jangili* can do nothing. With Papa Tembo the Ritual of the Night does not work. He is a spirit *tembo*, a spirit elephant. One day he will destroy us all.'

'Ritual of the Night?' asked Hyram.

'It is the magic of the *jangili*, the men who kill *tembo* for profit.'

'Ah,' said Hyram, his interest aroused. His eyes

caught Mike's, but once again Mike signalled him not to pursue the matter.

'Perhaps we can help,' Mike offered. 'If this elephant really is a rogue, a man-killer, then I may be prepared to track him and shoot him for you.'

Hyram's mouth dropped open in surprise. He stared hard at Mike but thought better about saying anything.

'Huh,' Kibasa snorted. 'Many men have tried.'

He fell silent for a moment. His face registered deep suspicion.

'Why would an *mzungu* want to help us anyway?' he asked, finally. 'What do you want in return?'

'Should we want anything?' Mike responded.

Kibasa's answer was scornful.

'The *wazungu* always want something. We have learned this well over our lifetimes. White men draw lines on maps and say, "This land is our land, this land is your land." Once all land was Maasai land. Now we are told where we can go and where we cannot. "Here," the *wazungu* say, "you cannot graze your cattle. Here you cannot build *manyattas*. Here you must pay taxes."'

'You're out of date,' Mike replied. 'You've had your own government for thirty years. Your own people.'

'Hah,' grunted Kibasa. '*Wazungu* government, not ours. Black skins now, but white men underneath. And white men always want something. You are here now in my home. You would not be here unless you wanted something.'

'All right. We have come for a reason. But it is only information we want. Nothing more.'

'What information?'

'We are looking for a man. His name is Laurens van der Wel. You know this man?'

Kibasa's face betrayed nothing.

'Perhaps,' he said, after a long pause.

The faces of the other Maasai showed no reaction either, but their very stillness at the mention of van der Wel's name gave the night a sudden tension.

Hyram felt the hairs on the back of his neck begin to tingle. The atmosphere surrounding them changed abruptly and he became acutely aware of the strangeness of where he was. The fire danced deep shadows on the long, red-robed figures of the Maasai, and their features, transformed by shifting light, suddenly seemed more savage, more primevally alien, than before. For a split second he felt a jolt of fear as the knowledge took root that they were in a very different world. A world which had changed little in thousands of years. A world of magic and ancient savagery where life meant little.

Had they made an error coming here? Perhaps Benny was wrong. Perhaps these people would not be disposed to help. Perhaps they viewed them as enemies. Perhaps, even, they were in van der Wel's pay.

He glanced around, nervously. The fire glinted on the wicked points of the tribesmen's spears. The shadows danced. The silence of the huge African night became oppressive.

Who would know if he and Mike and Benny were simply to disappear? They had not passed another soul since leaving Makayune. No one knew where they were. No one would look for them for days or even weeks. No one would care.

Hyram shivered. He felt very small, very insignificant and very vulnerable.

He glanced quickly at Mike to see if the same thoughts were going through his head. He seemed not to have noticed the tension and was as relaxed as before.

Kibasa broke the silence.

'So what are you saying? If we help you find van der Wel, you will kill Papa Tembo?'

'That is the bargain,' Mike replied, quietly. 'I can find him more easily than you. Your methods have not worked but my guns will.'

The headman rose to his feet.

'Wait here!' he ordered. 'I will talk with my people.'

He signalled to the other Maasai. They rose, one by one, and followed him. They disappeared into the darkness between the huts, on feet so silent they seemed to glide, ghost-like, into the gloom.

'J-e-e-e-z,' Hyram whispered, with a long exhalation of breath. 'I got to tell you something, Taylor.'

'What?'

'I got to tell you that these guys give me the heebie-jeebies, that's what. Where the hell's Benny? Let's get out of here.'

'Benny's guarding the Land Rover. And what do you mean "get out of here"? We're just getting somewhere.'

'Yes, I know we are. And I know just where we're getting to. We're getting to having a spear or two between our ears, that's where. Come on, let's move.'

He started to scramble awkwardly to his feet.

'Oh, for goodness' sake, Hyram, sit down. There's nothing wrong.'

'Nothing wrong? Did you see those guys' faces when you mentioned van der Wel's name?'

'Yes, of course I did. Nothing. They showed nothing.'

'Exactly. Show nothing and you're hiding something. Didn't you ever play poker? They're in van der Wel's pay. We've walked into a trap.'

'Rubbish. They're playing their cards close to their chests, that's all. They're deciding why we're looking for van der Wel now. Then they'll see whether they can get any more out of the bargain.'

'And that's another thing I want to talk to you about. What do you think you're playing at, offering to shoot elephants? I've come halfway round the world to save them and you're going to goddamn shoot them.'

'One. Shoot one.'

'That's one too many. You're a traitor, Taylor. A goddamn traitor. And, what's more, if we don't get out of here quick-sharp you're going to be a dead traitor. Which don't bother me at all except I'll be dead with you.'

'Hyram, think for a minute before you open your mouth, will you? Isn't one elephant worth it if they tell us where van der Wel is? It's one elephant in exchange for hundreds if we put a stop to his trade. Our chances of finding a man like that without help are nil. What's the death of one elephant? This is Africa. At this very moment thousands of animals are dying out there. Everything is eating everything else. Calm down and get a sense of proportion.'

'If you say "This is Africa" one more time to me I'll get that goddamn elephant gun and blow your goddamn head off. Then there'll be one less Great White Hunter. That should make the world a better place. Shooting an elephant doesn't.'

'I keep reminding you where you are, Hyram, because people like you always bring your prejudices with you and try to ram them down our throats. What seems right in your country isn't necessarily right here. You heard the man. This elephant destroys their livelihoods. You step out of your front door in New York, walk ten paces into a shop and buy all the food you need. These people have their cattle and their gardens and nothing else. They have to grow everything they need, animal or vegetable. If something destroys those things, they starve. They watch their children die. I don't like to shoot any animal, but sometimes it's unavoidable. And on top of everything else you just watched him kill a man. The elephant's a rogue. So keep your smart city attitudes to yourself. They don't belong here. And sit down and shut up, they're coming back.'

Deflated, Hyram slumped irritably back onto the ground.

The Maasai filed back into the clearing. They remained standing, as though what they had to say would take little time.

The headman studied Mike and Hyram before he spoke.

'We have decided. The man, van der Wel, he is not our enemy, so we have no reason to help you.'

I knew it, Hyram thought, *they're in his pay.*

'But,' the headman continued, 'nor is he our friend, so we owe him nothing.'

Mike nodded.

'We know of him. We know where he may be. Return with the tusks of Papa Tembo and we will talk again. That is all. Sleep now. You are welcome here. For now.'

And with that he spun abruptly on his heels and swept away. The other men melted into their huts. Within seconds Mike and Hyram were alone.

'Doesn't believe in small talk, does he?' Hyram observed.

'He doesn't trust us. The Maasai don't trust anyone. We're all lower forms of life to them.'

'I, on the other hand,' said Hyram, 'trust them completely. I don't know where you're going to sleep, Taylor, but I'm going to sleep in the Land Rover, with all the doors locked and a gun in my hand. And if I had a few landmines I'd surround the Land Rover with them too.'

'Please yourself. I'm staying here by the fire.'

'Good.'

Hyram started to walk away.

'I hope they sneak out in the middle of the night and dismember you. Cut you up into small pieces while you're still conscious – bit by bit, very slowly, very brutally. You're a rat traitor fink schmuck. Shoot a goddamn elephant indeed. We'll goddamn see about goddamn that. Jeez, I never thought . . .'

His voice faded away into the night.

'Goodnight, Hyram,' said Mike, mildly.

FOURTEEN

*'There is mystery behind that masked grey visage,
and ancient life force, delicate and mighty,
awesome and enchanted, commanding the silence
ordinarily reserved for mountain peaks, great
fires and the sea.'*

Peter Matthiessen, *The Tree Where Man Was Born*, 1972

The elephants ran, without pause and in an arrow-straight line, for about six kilometres. Even with the Land Rover's great strength and agility Matt was unable to keep up with them. Dodging tussocks and protruding rocks, he bounced and crashed the vehicle after the herd. His passengers were thrown violently from side to side and periodically hurled upwards out of their seats.

Eventually, with the Land Rover now half a kilometre behind them, the herd turned, ascended a low, wooded slope and vanished between the trees.

'They've gone to hide,' Alison remarked. Matt turned the Land Rover slightly and started to head towards the slope. 'Something frightened them and now they're hiding.'

'I don't know,' Matt replied. 'This is very strange behaviour. There's not much elephants are frightened of, though they're very careful when they've got new calves.'

'Except man, of course,' John Blake added. 'They've learned to be frightened of man. Like everything else in the world.'

'They're not frightened of us, are they?' Alison asked. 'I mean, I know they're not in normal circumstances, but perhaps, if Cleopatra's going to give birth soon, they just decided they needed to get away from us.'

'No. They don't even notice us any more. This is the fourteenth year of the study now. We're just part of the scenery to them.'

Matt slowed down as they reached the foot of the slope.

'It was too sudden,' he said. 'One minute they were relaxed, the next minute they were running. Anyway, perhaps we'll find out now.'

He put the Land Rover into bottom gear, ground quietly up to the tree-line and switched off the engine. In the hush that followed they could hear the elephants rustling through the trees.

And something else.

'Listen,' Alison said.

They climbed out of the Land Rover and stood in silence. Above the noise of the moving herd was another sound. A long, low breathy rumbling. So deep a sound that it was felt, rather than heard. Deep as the sound of the deepest pipe in a great cathedral organ, it rumbled and groaned through the trees, rattling their leaves.

It settled as a vibration that trembled through the listeners' bodies, disquieting and disturbing.

'What's that?' asked Alison anxiously. 'What on earth is that?'

Urrrrrrr. Pause. *Urrrrrrr.* Pause. *Urrrrrrr.*

Intermittent but rhythmic, the sound pulsed out from the trees. A call of heart-rending distress. Of solitary pain. The call of a great beast in extremity.

'It's another elephant,' John Blake said, quietly. 'It's injured.'

'Oh.' Alison's hand flew to her mouth. 'Oh, listen to it. The poor, poor thing. What are we going to do?'

'They heard it,' said Matt, wonderingly. 'From six kilometres away, they heard it. We can barely hear it now, but they heard it.'

He started to walk towards the trees.

'Where do you think you're going?' John Blake asked.

'I'm going to take a look.'

'No you're not. Stay where you are. You can't go blundering in there. The whole herd will be on edge. There's no knowing what they'll do. You go marching into the middle of things and they'll just pick you up and throw you out of the way.'

'But Dad,' Alison said, shocked, 'we've got to do something. Perhaps we can help. We can't just stand here listening to the poor thing. It's in terrible pain.'

'I didn't say we weren't going to do anything. We'll go and see what's happened, but we'll go carefully and we'll go prepared.'

He went to the back of the Land Rover, opened

the door and unclipped the semi-automatic rifle from its rack. Then he unlocked the ammunition box, took out a cartridge of nine bullets and clipped it into the gun.

'Precaution,' he said, defensively, as he noticed his daughter's alarmed glance. 'I don't intend to shoot anything unless I have to. But if we get into trouble we might be glad of this.'

'I know, I know,' said Alison.

'Now, we'll go in. Very gently. They know we're here, of course, and they know who we are. But something like this will have made them very unpredictable. You two get behind me. And stay together. No matter what you see or what happens, stay with me, and stay behind the gun.'

'Right.'

They walked to the edge of the trees and entered the copse.

'Now, slow and delicate,' John Blake ordered as he began to creep forward.

The terrible groaning continued and grew louder as they slid through the trees. It was joined now by loud gruntings from the adult cows, and anxious snortings and squealings from the calves. Ahead of them they began to discern the grey shapes of the herd. They were gathered together, moving slowly about, trunks in the air, milling around a single elephant who was standing stock-still.

'Oh no!' Alison whispered, recognizing the figure as they approached. 'Look, it's Daffodil. You can see his broken tusk. It's poor Daffodil. What's happened to him?'

'He's standing up at least. Perhaps it's not as bad as we thought,' Matt observed. 'Can we get a bit closer?'

They crept forward a pace at a time, taking immense care where they placed their feet so no sound should upset the herd.

Daffodil continued to groan with agony, and made no attempt to move. He seemed fastened to one spot. The herd shuffled around him, the cows reaching out with their trunks to touch him and calm him. They grunted and rumbled reassurance as the tips of their trunks explored his body for injury.

Matt moved slightly to one side to get a better view.

Once again Alison was struck by the strangely human quality of these great, primeval beasts. Solicitous and anxious, the grey bulks moved about and discussed the event almost as a group of people gathered at the scene of an accident would do.

Matt drew in his breath with a sharp hissing sound.

'What is it?' whispered Alison.

'I can see what's happened. He's in a trap. Get where you can see his back right leg.'

Alison and her father moved to one side and joined Matt.

'Look there,' he said.

Daffodil was holding his right leg out limply behind him. Blood was running down from just below his knee and had stained the grass around his foot. A thin, silver wire stretched back from his leg to a tall sapling. The animal, baffled and in pain, periodically pulled on the wire and groaned as it bit deeper into his flesh. The sapling swayed as he pulled.

John Blake hissed through his teeth.

'He's in a snare, a classic snare,' he whispered. 'Look, the wire goes back from the sapling. He could have pulled that out of the ground easily, but it's fastened again further back.'

Matt and Alison followed the glinting wire with their eyes from Daffodil's leg to the swaying sapling and along to where it was coiled and knotted around the massive trunk of an ancient fig tree.

'The sapling was just the spring,' their father continued. 'They make a noose of the wire and conceal it with grass or leaves. Then they run the wire along the ground to a trigger, just a piece of wood driven into the ground to hold the wire in place. Then they bend a sapling over and tie the wire to it. The elephants walk into the noose, pull the trigger out of the ground and the sapling springs up and tightens the noose. A classic trick. The poor things just starve to death. Then, weeks later, someone will come along and harvest the tusks.'

'It's barbaric,' Alison said. Her voice shook with anger. 'Poor Daffodil. What are we going to do?'

'What you and Matt are going to do is go back to the Land Rover. I'll be along in a minute.'

'Go back? What do you mean, go back? We've got to help him. We've got to release him.'

'We can't. The herd wouldn't let us near him.'

'I don't understand,' Alison said. 'Can't we drive the others off? Fire some shots in the air or something?'

'It won't work, Alison. They won't leave Daffodil. They'll attack us. We wouldn't stand a chance.'

'But what's the alternative?' Her voice was beginning to rise with alarm. 'We can't leave him here to starve to death. What are you saying?'

'Come on, Alison,' said Matt gently, taking her arm. 'Let's do as Dad says.'

Alison looked at him wonderingly. There was a long pause. Slowly realization dawned.

'No!' she said, her voice harsh with shock. 'No! You can't be thinking that. I can't believe you would be thinking that.'

'There's no other way. You said yourself, we can't leave him to starve.'

'You're going to shoot him. You're going to shoot Daffodil. Oh, Dad.'

Her eyes filled with tears.

'It's quick and painless,' Matt said. 'The other way doesn't bear thinking about.'

'No. No, I won't let you do it. I won't.'

'Look,' her father insisted, 'we can't do anything. Even if we could release the wire from the tree we could never get near enough to free it from his leg. He's finished. Go back. Now. I want you two in the Land Rover with the engine running when I get there.'

Abruptly Alison tore her arm away from Matt's grasp. Before anyone could even think of stopping her, she spun away from them and darted out through the trees towards the herd.

'Oh no!' Matt gasped.

John Blake's heart missed a beat.

'Dear God,' he whispered. 'Of all the stupid things . . .'

Immediately, hearing the sound of her approach, the adult elephants began a loud snorting and grunting. The young calves squealed in response and huddled against their mothers' sides.

When Matt and his father followed they found

that Alison had stopped at the edge of the clearing, less than twenty metres from the herd. The elephants, momentarily confused by the sudden appearance of humans, seemed unsure what to do. They moved slightly closer to Daffodil, as though to protect him from the new threat.

'Stand absolutely still,' John Blake hissed to his children. He held the gun diagonally across his body, pointing upwards, ready to fire a warning volley into the air. 'Matt, get hold of Alison. Keep her there.'

He moved so that he was standing in front of them. His eyes quickly sought out the matriarch, Queen Victoria. She was on the far side of the herd. Although the others were now huffing and stamping and flapping their ears in startled anger, he knew that the real threat was from her. The rest would wait for her signal.

'That was the most stupid thing you've ever done,' Matt snarled in a whisper at his sister. 'I just hope you live to regret it.'

He was gripping Alison firmly by the shoulders. He could feel her trembling as the terrible realization that she had put them all in mortal danger took hold in her mind.

John Blake started to back up slowly, forcing Matt and Alison to edge back too. He saw Queen Victoria's great head and trunk raise up high into the air as she sniffed them out, then, locating them, she started to push her way between the others. The herd parted, shuffling and bellowing, to let her through.

She emerged, massive and baleful and deeply frightening, and placed herself protectively between her herd and the humans. Then she stopped and regarded them.

The humans stopped too, pinned to immobility by the awesome spectacle of this great beast fixing them in a steady, fearless gaze of suspicious anger.

John Blake found that his hands were gripping the rifle so tightly that his muscles were knotting. He forced himself to relax. Very slowly, almost imperceptibly, he began to inch the rifle up to his shoulder.

'Now,' he whispered, 'she's making up her mind. If she charges, run. Run like hell.'

A heavy, ominous silence had fallen as the elephants waited to see what the matriarch would do. Even Daffodil had quietened, aware through his pain and distress that a threat faced the others too. Several seconds ticked slowly by.

Victoria pawed the ground. A great foot thumped the earth hollowly and slid back with a deeply menacing scrape. Then again. Then her ears flapped, once only, hard back against her neck with a sharp, loud crack.

'That's it. She's coming at us.' John Blake flicked the rifle up the last couple of centimetres to his shoulder. 'Get out of here. Now! I'll try and frighten her off.'

Matt swung Alison around and pushed her hard towards the protection of the trees.

'Move!' he commanded. 'Quickly.'

John Blake took aim at a point about six inches above Victoria's head, praying that a single bullet whistling past her would change her mind.

Then Victoria started to move too, slowly at first, but rapidly gathering speed. Her head rose in challenge and her ears pivoted out from her head like sails. She opened her mouth and gave a deafening bellow. Her feet came high up off the ground as she pranced into the terrifying display of full charge.

Matt and Alison, now well into the protection of the trees, stopped and turned at the sound.

Alison screamed in fear as she saw the elephant bearing down on her father.

'Dad!' she shouted. 'Come on! Get away from there!'

John Blake stood his ground. In the split second he had for thought it was obvious that Victoria was enraged beyond heeding a warning shot. He would have to drop her.

He lowered the sight of the gun and took aim directly between Victoria's eyes, his finger beginning to assert a tiny pressure on the trigger.

And, because he knew the herd so well, because their personalities, their habits and quirks had become so affectionately familiar to him, because in a small way their triumphs and failures had become a part of his life, he paused, his finger arrested by a brief flash of anguish passing through his mind.

The disappointment that he, of all people, should be the one to end this animal's life.

The tiniest of pauses only – hardly measurable as time at all.

But long enough, as John Blake well knew, to have killed him.

Except that in the pause the picture changed.

Amazingly, Victoria stopped.

She literally skidded to a halt, dust swirling up around her feet. She snorted once, softly, then her raised head slowly turned to one side, peering into the trees away to John Blake's right. Something had caught her attention, something more important than puny man.

At that moment Matt and Alison became aware of a soft rustling and cracking from behind them. The sound of branches and trees being pushed to one side. The herd began to grunt and snuffle again in excitement.

'What is it?' Alison whispered.

'Shush. I don't know.'

Victoria, to John Blake's astonishment, began to back off, silently. She shook her head gently from side to side as she went. The other elephants began to move slowly away from Daffodil. They had all fallen quiet again too, as though they listened expectantly to the approaching noise.

Daffodil groaned once in the ensuing quiet.

Matt turned and looked hard in the direction of the sound. The rustling and the cracks of breaking trees grew louder.

'Look! Over there!' Alison whispered, gripping Matt's arm tightly.

Matt's eyes followed her gaze.

Slowly, only a few metres behind them, a massive figure was beginning to emerge. A figure so huge, so awesome that it stopped the watchers' breath. Head down, the figure moved easily and without pause through the trees, pushing them to one side as though they did not exist, inexorable as a slowly rolling boulder grinding a path down a mountain.

Matt exhaled with a soft hiss. He took hold of Alison's hand and pulled her silently back until they were behind the trunk of a baobab tree, out of the path of the approaching figure.

'It's a huge bull. Just look at the size of him,' he whispered.

Alison nodded, too awed to reply, too stunned by the immensity and quiet power of the great beast to do anything but stare in fascination.

And suddenly she realized that the strangest of things had happened. Only a few seconds ago they had been running in panic from Queen Victoria's charge. Only a few seconds ago she had screamed with fear at the knowledge of the great danger they were in. Only a few seconds ago they had all believed that they were facing death.

Now, oddly, as this great bull elephant, this most powerful and potentially dangerous of all creatures on earth, approached, she found herself to be calm. Her trembling had ceased, the fear which had coursed through her body was gone, the terrible dread in the pit of her stomach had stilled.

And more than that.

As she watched the great figure slide by, like a grey wall, within a few metres of where she stood, her senses told her that everything else had calmed too. Matt, standing beside her, was breathing quietly and normally. Through the trees she could see that her father had moved away to one side. The herd had moved off too. They stood quietly grouped together on the far side of the clearing. Even Daffodil had ceased pulling on the cruel wire and groaning, and now stood quite still. The pain and distress which had tautened his body had gone. He stood almost, it seemed, relaxed.

Somehow this slow-moving, immense presence had taken, had *absorbed* the fear from the day and replaced it with a soft, enfolding blanket of confidence. Of calm, unhurried, but complete, power and control.

Suddenly, instinctively, all the players in this small but desperate drama knew their parts.

Suddenly the very air around them told them that everything was going to be all right.

Alison, almost without thinking, stepped out from behind the tree and began to follow the bull. This time, though they could give no reason for it, neither Matt nor her father made any effort to stop her or follow her.

Later, when the magic was dispelled and cold logic applied, that was all they would ever be able to say.

It felt right.

And so John and Matt Blake were able only to watch in quiet wonder as the two figures proceeded towards the clearing, the vast bulk of the bull dwarfing the small, fragile girl who followed.

The elephant emerged on to the open ground. He padded softly across to Daffodil and touched him gently with his trunk, rumbling a message of reassurance. Daffodil grunted softly in reply.

Alison stood quietly at the edge of the clearing, watching, waiting. On the other side, less than twenty metres from her, the herd shuffled and muttered encouragement, but made no move to approach.

The bull lowered his trunk to Daffodil's stricken and bleeding leg and began to trace the course of the trap. Exploring delicately with the tip of his trunk he followed the line of wire back along its length until he reached the bent sapling. Almost carelessly he lowered his head, sank one of his huge tusks into the soft earth and, with an effortless flick of his head, ripped the tree out by its roots. It fell to the ground and the terrible, biting tension of the wire loosened. Daffodil moved his hurt leg forward slightly in relief, but then groaned again as the tension was taken up by the wire's main anchor around the huge fig tree.

Alison began to walk towards Daffodil as the great bull moved away. Later, when she thought about the enormity of what she had done, there would be fear.

Never approach a wild animal.

It had been drilled into her since birth.

And never, never, never approach an injured animal if you value your life.

But they were instructions for another time. Here, in this place, in these circumstances, there was no room for logic. Here there was only one thing to do. And everybody, animal and human alike, knew it.

She began to whisper as she neared Daffodil.

'It's all right. Don't be frightened. Don't worry.'

Daffodil responded by flapping his ears gently. He showed no alarm, no aggression, just stood quietly in his pain.

Alison walked right up to the stricken beast and stood beside him, still whispering gently to him.

John and Matt Blake held their breaths in awe at what they witnessed.

The bull had now reached the fig tree and was standing head-on to it. He rocked slightly backward then, with an almost disdainful lurch, thudded one of his tusks deep into the fibrous body of the tree. With barely more than a casual flick of his head he tore a long, deep gash vertically in the trunk, catching the coils of wire under the end of his tusk. The wire snapped as though it were cotton and twanged away to writhe like a broken-backed snake along the ground.

Daffodil was freed from his prison. Almost.

Alison immediately sank to her knees beside Daffodil's bleeding leg. She knew she had only seconds to do this before the animal realized he was free and began to move away. She plunged her fingers into the crimson gash circling his leg, located the wire buried deep in his flesh, hooked her fingernails behind it and pulled hard. Miraculously the terrible noose loosened instantly and she pulled it wide, slipping it down onto the ground. Then she jumped to her feet and stepped back away from Daffodil.

Just in time. For at that second the elephant began to move. Tentatively at first, as though he expected the pain still to be there, he inched his leg forward. Then, meeting no resistance, he gave a bellow of what seemed to the onlookers to be pure joy and set off at a limping gallop across the clearing to rejoin the herd. They welcomed him with a great cacophony of hoots and bellows and grunts and rumbles. Briefly they fussed him and questioned him and then, with astonishing speed and ease, they left, melting away into the trees.

Still caught in the magic of the moment Alison watched their departure. Within seconds they were lost to sight but she continued to stare, happy with relief, at the place where they had been, listening to the sounds of their rumblings and squealings and huffings as they faded rapidly away into the distance.

Soon even their noise was gone.

Then gradually, in the deep silence that followed,

Alison felt the skin on the back of her neck begin to prickle. Without turning she knew what was causing it.

She was being watched.

The great bull was still there. Silent, motionless, he was watching her.

Slowly, very slowly, she turned. Her father, she noticed, was still standing at the edge of the clearing, in the shadow of the trees. Matt was standing just behind him.

Even though cold reality was now beginning to seep back into her mind, there was still no fear. Wonder, rather, at the strangeness of it all. What she had just done was beyond belief. More, it was suicidal. Yet here she was, still alive. Here were her father and brother making no move to join her.

It didn't make sense. It was against all the laws of survival, against all the laws of Africa.

She completed her turn and raised her eyes.

In the great noise of the departing herd the bull had approached unheard. He was standing very close to her, staring at her. So close that she was in the shadow of his immense head. So close she could hear his quiet, rhythmic breathing and smell the warm, sweet-grass scent of his breath.

They stood for long minutes regarding each other.

Minutes during which realization began to wash over Alison in waves. Minutes in which the spell began to fade and be replaced by a growing unease.

What was this great, silent beast thinking? What did he see from those soft, liquid eyes?

What was he going to do, this huge, primeval animal who could kill her, in an instant, with one careless tap of his trunk?

A sudden terror shot through her body and she gasped, involuntarily, with fear. Her hands began to tremble uncontrollably and she felt her legs beginning to give way. Suddenly the immensity of this motionless, implacable beast was too much.

He was too big, too fearsome and too strange.

She felt her legs begin to buckle and she sank to her knees.

'Dad, Matt,' she whimpered. 'Help me!'

The two men started to move out into the clearing. The elephant reacted immediately. He swung his head to the side, rumbled a low, deep warning and, stamping his foot, took a step towards Alison.

The men stopped, frozen into uncertainty.

Alison was sobbing with fear now. The elephant was so close she could have reached out and touched his trunk. His vast, grey bulk loomed over her, blotting out everything. There was no sky, no trees, no light. Only greyness and terror.

And then the elephant rumbled again.

But this time it was a different sound. Not the sound of warning he had given to her father and Matt, but a soft rumble of reassurance.

The sound he had made to Daffodil earlier.

An unmistakably gentle sound.

Through her tears Alison looked up at the elephant's great head towering above her. For a second their eyes met and in that brief, tiny meeting all her fears were stilled. The eyes held no threat, no anger, no danger.

Rather, Alison thought, a gentle, quizzical wonderment, as though the great beast was as awed at the strangeness of their proximity as she was.

Slowly the elephant reached out his trunk towards her and, with infinite gentleness, touched her hair. So delicate was the touch that Alison barely felt it.

And then the moment was over.

The trunk retracted. The elephant grunted and began to back gently away. He glanced momentarily at the two men standing in silent wonder at the clearing's edge, then he turned and padded softly away into the trees.

Alison watched him go, torn now between wonder and relief. She remained on her knees, waiting for her father and brother to join her.

The elephant's odour lingered heavy in her nostrils.

She reached up her trembling hand and touched her hair. It was slightly damp where the velvet wetness of the trunk had passed over it.

The hair would soon dry of course, and the odour fade.

But that didn't matter.

His touch, and the smell of him had, in that brief moment, entered her heart.

And would, she knew, remain there for ever.

FIFTEEN

*'. . . a shadow insatiable of splendid appearances,
of frightful realities; a shadow darker than the
shadow of the night . . .'*

Joseph Conrad, *Heart of Darkness*, 1902

Laurens van der Wel's hands trembled slightly as he
clipped the last of the guns into its place in the rack
at the back of the truck.

His tension had nothing to do with the loading
of the guns and the ropes and the axes. The instru-
ments of killing and dismemberment were too familiar,
too much a part of his life to cause excitement any
more.

Not even the report of the sighting of the herd
and the thought of the coming slaughter was sufficient
now, after a lifetime of bloodletting, to cause more
than a small feeling of satisfaction when he made his
preparations. He was a workman laying out his tools,
that was all.

No. It was the other piece of information his scout
had imparted that caused his excitement.

'And, *bwana*,' the scout had said, 'with them, for a time, was the big one, Papa Tembo.'

The first sighting of this elusive and hated figure for months.

Perhaps, this time, they would come face to face at last.

He snapped open the catch on the ammunition box and checked inside. The curved clips of bullets, stacked in orderly rows, gleamed dully back at him. The heavy, satin greyness of them, offsetting the bright brass of the top bullet, was a sight which always brought a small smile of satisfaction to his lips. He reached his hand into the box and touched the cold metal, caressing the clips with his fingertips.

Perhaps this time . . .

But then he stopped. The smile faded and he slammed the lid down sharply.

He snorted with annoyance. He was being self-indulgent, building up too much hope. That was not wise.

A sighting meant nothing. This was a clever beast. There had been many sightings before, many hurried preparations, many, many disappointments. This one would likely be no different. When they found the herd the big one would be long gone. That was the way it always was.

Expect not to find him, then if you do, the pleasure will be greater. That was the way to think.

Sometimes, over the years, he had even begun to feel that his men were right. That the beast could not be killed. That he was a phantom who could appear and disappear at will. A shade, built of air and mist and grey volcanic dust, like the shifting vapours which swirled on the slopes of Ol Doinyo Lengai.

Nonsense, of course. Ignorant, primitive superstition. The mythic, mumbo-jumbo of stupid, uneducated men.

And yet.

He paused, listening to the soft murmurs of the men as they began to gather round their dusk fires outside the compound fence.

As the harsh light of African day begins to fade, and the shadows gather, so too fades the confidence of logic.

The day has Land Rovers and trucks and guns, radios and aeroplanes and the comforting proximity of towns and cities. The confident apparatus of twentieth-century men.

At night their value leaks away as time reverses a million, million years and magic steps out of the gloom.

Night, African night, returns a man, even a man of the twentieth century, to what he was at the dawn of time. A puny, naked interloper, fighting for his place. A place where the hyenas, the 'cattle of the night', watch in constant, macabre vigil for him, waiting to crunch his bones.

At night it is easier to believe. Easier to see the Mbugwe, the witch people of Manyara, shrieking vengeance as they ride the hyenas. Easier to see the lycanthropes, the lion-men, the leopard-men, the elephant-men, men who have taken animal form and roam the vast plains of the *veldt* settling their daytime, human scores.

Laurens van der Wel shuddered as he looked out of the back of the truck and heard the men speaking.

111

They would soon, he knew, be performing the 'Ritual of the Night' – the dark, ancient ceremony which would assure them of success and safety in the hunt.

His lip curled slightly in contempt.

He could not believe in their magic, of course.

What white man could?

But, in his heart of hearts, in the darkness, surrounded by great, silent plains stalked by creatures of prehistoric antiquity, what man, white or black, could not?

He climbed out of the back of the truck, hoisted the heavy tailgate upward and slammed it into position. The hollow clang of metal echoed out into the darkness and the chains rattled dully as he slipped the locking pins into place.

The men outside the fence quietened as they heard him.

He smiled. No matter what their magic, their ancient sorcery, they were still afraid of him.

That was what really mattered. Their spells would not affect the hunt at all.

Their fear of him, that was the vital component of success. That was what would garner the ivory.

He limped across the dusty volcanic earth of the compound towards his house, set back deep in a fold of the rocks at the end of the depression. A pale, insipid moon cast a faint light onto the dark bulk of Ol Doinyo Lengai, rising steeply behind the house. The cool evening air condensing on its hot slopes shrouded it in a slow-swirling cloak of diaphanous light, ghostly and strange. The ever-present dust clouds, swept into constant motion by the gases and steam vents, shot dark, flitting shadows through the mist. Shapes stepped out of the pale light and back again.

He stopped briefly and watched.

A man could imagine many things in these phantoms. Once, in a long-ago sunset, he had even thought he had seen Papa Tembo sliding silently down the mountainside through the clouds. His great bulk had been lit red by the deep glow of two setting suns.

It had been a trick of the light, of course. The dust clouds had refracted the sunset through a million prisms and thrown a twin, phantom sun onto a screen of swirling mist and dust particles.

But the memory had stayed with him, had returned in sleep to haunt him, jolting him awake, sweating, in the low hours of the night.

For the vision was not his alone, but a vision woven into the folklore of Africa.

The African knows that the world is coming to an end and knows the signs that will precede the end. In the world's final days the animals will eat the land into desert and then begin to disappear. Fighting and war will increase as land becomes scarcer for men, and the sky will darken with great clouds of birds travelling further and further for food.

On the last day two suns will appear on the horizon, one in the east, one in the west. At their final setting, in the ultimate dusk, the Child of Man will appear for the last time to signal the end of all mankind.

And, as the suns finally sink below the rim of the world, the earth will shrivel and all will be gone.

Laurens van der Wel smiled at the story. Though he scorned the myths of Africa, the world could end at any time for all he cared. Just so long as, on that last day, he would have a final chance to come face to face with Papa Tembo.

He turned away from the slopes and looked out across the dark plains to the east. Far in the distance the moonlight caught the black bulk of Gelai, standing guard on the lonely, sulphur sea of Lake Natron, and away to the south-east Kitumbeine loomed heavily up from the ancient, shrouded haze.

Somewhere out there, in that dark triangle of plain, was Papa Tembo.

'Perhaps tomorrow,' Laurens van der Wel whispered to himself.

Outside the compound fence the *jangili*, the hunters, listened as van der Wel shuffled back to his house, then, when they heard the slam of his front door, they returned to their preparations.

The oldest and most senior, the Mchawi, the witch doctor, sat at the head of the group gathered around the fire. A piece of old, rotting sacking, stained dark with generations of blood, lay on the ground beside him, tied roughly with bush string. Beside it lay a long, wickedly pointed knife, its slim blade glinting redly in the flames of the fire.

A small, blackened cauldron sat at the fire's edge, its contents simmering gently and seeping an acrid, corrosive stench into the air.

The men had painted their faces with the yellow, sulphurous mud which stained the black volcanic earth of the escarpment. The fire caught the luminosity of it, so their faces glowed, ghost-like, in the night and floated, seemingly detached from their bodies, as they swayed to the sound of the Mchawi's low chant.

The men joined in with the chant, murmuring the ancient words, invoking the spirits of the land where tomorrow they would hunt. Seeking the permission without which there could be no success.

Then the Mchawi stood and walked over to a low acacia tree. Snapping off one of the long thorns from its branches, he knelt and scratched a square about a metre across in the dry earth in the tree's shadow. With infinite care he cleared the patch. Every blade of grass, every fallen thorn, every flower, every dried and withered leaf, every stone was removed until nothing remained but dust.

Standing, he reached into the pouch at his waist and pulled from it a handful of millet seed. Holding his hand in a fist he slowly trickled the seeds into the square. Then he turned and took his place again at the fire.

In the morning he would inspect the seeds. If the spirits were happy for them to hunt, the millet would be undisturbed and the elephants would have remained on the land where they had been seen. If the seeds were gone, the spirits had withheld their permission and the hunt would be doomed.

He turned his attention now to the bundle of sacking, slowly undoing the binding and peeling off the filthy layers of cloth. As he opened it, another foul stench began to permeate the air, so vile it displaced the acid vapours steaming up from the cauldron. The stench strengthened as the final layer was removed and a shapeless, putrescent lump of meat was revealed. It writhed and boiled with white maggots, sickening and obscene.

Seemingly impervious to the vileness of it, the

Mchawi placed the meat on the ground in front of him and began to slice slivers from it, passing them round to the seated men. Maggots crawled frantically over his hands and wriggled on the meat he handed out. The men ignored them and chewed solemnly, happy in the knowledge that tomorrow there would be no dangers in the hunt. Having eaten of the heart of an elephant, tomorrow they would be invisible to the herd and could kill them with impunity.

Finally the Mchawi reached his knife forward, slipped the long blade through the handle of the cauldron and lifted it off the fire.

The *jangili* rose, picked up their bundles of arrows and, one by one, approached the pot and plunged the cruelly barbed tips into the steaming liquid.

Tomorrow, of course, the *bwana* would give them guns.

But guns, as they all knew, did not always do the job. Guns sometimes only wounded and the elephant could escape.

From this pale bubbling liquid there was no escape.

Once an arrow tipped with the juice of the *acokanthera*, the shrubby dogbane, has pierced the skin there is no release but death.

'Aia,' said the Mchawi.

'Aia,' the men repeated.

So be it.

The preparations were made.

SIXTEEN

'A baby elephant is almost a perfect miniature of an adult except that it has no tusks and it tends to have more hair.'

Cynthia Moss, *Elephant Memories*, 1988

'What are you doing?'

'What do you mean, "What am I doing?" I'm getting my sleeping bag out of the tent. What does it look like I'm doing?'

'I can see that. What I mean is, what are you doing it *for*? I've just put the sleeping bags in the tent, and now you're dragging them out again.'

'I'm dragging *mine* out again. I'm not sleeping in the tent.'

'Please yourself. Get bitten to death by mosquitoes. Get eaten by lions. See if I care.'

'Just mind your own business. If I want to get eaten I will. If you want to sleep through the greatest event you're ever likely to see, then that's fine. Just don't expect me to miss it with you.'

'For heaven's sake,' John Blake snapped. 'You two

are getting on my nerves. You've done nothing but bicker all afternoon. Put a sock in it, the pair of you.'

'Well, I'm fed up with him,' Alison snapped back. 'Something wonderful happened today. We all saw it. I saved Daffodil's life and all Matt can do is go on about how stupid I was and how I put everyone in danger.'

'Well, so you did,' said Matt. 'The fact that things turned out all right was pure luck. If that bull hadn't turned up at just the right moment and calmed things down, we'd all be sitting counting white tiles on the walls of Nairobi morgue right now.'

Alison's voice quavered with emotion as she drew the argument to a close in the only way she could.

'Shut up, Matt!' she shouted. 'Just shut up, will you?'

And she stamped off away from the camp, dragging her sleeping bag behind her.

'That wasn't fair, Matt. She did what she had to do. We were doing the same. In the end the bull gave none of us any choice. He decided.'

'I know. What's your "scientific" report going to say about that?'

'Nothing much. Other than that I think we finally saw Papa Tembo. You know – that old bull they talk about? Would you believe, in all these years I've never seen him, he's so elusive. But elephants have been recorded many times as rescuing each other. There's nothing new in that. I'll give it a couple of lines in the diary. "5/10 injured in trap. Released by Male, herd unknown." That sort of thing.'

'Hm. And what would your private diary say, if you had one?'

'It would say that we were all upset about Daffodil, that we all had a bad fright, that we've all seen something for which we have no rational explanation and never will have, that we've all got very emotional and ratty and maybe we should all apologize to each other and go to bed. That sort of thing.'

'And that's as far as you're going to go?'

'Yup. And if you think that you can drag me into discussions about animals' "feelings" then you've another think coming. That's not science. You know I can't stand that. Animals act on instinct, that's all.'

' "There are more things in heaven and earth . . ." '

'Stop it,' said John Blake firmly, closing the discussion. 'Now go and look after Alison for a while. See if you can persuade her to go to bed. And try and prepare her for a disappointment. Hardly anyone has ever seen an elephant birth. When she's ready Cleopatra will go off somewhere very dark and very private. We'll see nothing until the calf's trotting along behind her. And anyway, we're almost out of food and petrol, so tomorrow we'll head back to Seronera and stock up. Let her know that too.'

Matt turned away and began to walk over to where Alison sat hunched against a tree. Then, changing his mind, he stopped, turned, went back to the tent and dragged his sleeping bag out.

John Blake shook his head resignedly and smiled.

Alison was crying gently.

Matt threw his sleeping bag down onto the ground, sat down beside his sister and put his arm around her shoulder.

'I'm sorry,' he said.

119

'So am I.'

'I know.'

'It was just such an awful day. Poor Daffodil. Bleeding and crying out. The pain must have been terrible. And Dad going to shoot him. I couldn't have stood that. Daffodil's twelve this year. I've known him most of my life. He was the first one born after we came out here. I wasn't even four then, so he was the first baby elephant I ever saw. I've seen him grow. I just couldn't have stood seeing him die.'

'I know. He'll be all right. The others will look after him now.'

'And that big bull. He touched me. He actually reached out and touched me. I looked into his eyes. Can you believe that happened?'

'I saw it. It happened.'

'For a moment I was so terrified. I thought I was going to die. And he knew. He knew I was frightened and he spoke to me. He told me it was all right. And he touched me.'

Her shoulders shook under Matt's arm with the emotion of it all. He hugged her reassuringly.

'It's all right. It's over. We all survived. There's nothing to be frightened of now.'

'No, that's not it. You don't understand. I'm not frightened of him any more. I'm not frightened of any of them. It's something else. Ever since I looked into his eyes, for some reason, I don't know why, I've felt so sad. So terribly, terribly sad. There was something in his eyes. I don't know what it was. But whatever it was, it's hurt me.'

'You're right. I don't understand. But I'll tell you something. If you don't stop crying there's not much point in us sitting out here all night hoping to see Cleopatra give birth. You'll see nothing for tears.'

Alison looked up at him.

'What do you mean, "us"?' she enquired, rubbing her eyes with the back of her hand.

'I'm here now, aren't I? I might as well stay. It's too much trouble going back to the tent now.'

Alison smiled.

'Thanks.'

'You're welcome. I wouldn't want to miss "the greatest event I'm ever likely to see", now would I?'

'All right. Don't rub it in. I've said I'm sorry for snapping.'

'Anyway, Dad says we won't see anything. No one in the entire history of the world has ever seen an elephant give birth, no one ever will, and if anyone ever does Dad won't believe it and he'll call it "anecdotal evidence" because he wasn't there and if he wasn't there it couldn't have happened.'

'Yes,' said Alison. 'It's called "science".'

'Hm. But the light on the horizon is that no one's told the elephants. So let's creep down towards the copse and see what we can see.'

They took up a position halfway down the hillside and sat down to watch.

The elephants had calmed and were slowly positioning themselves for sleep, rumbling grumpily and shuffling the young into the centre of the small thicket they had chosen. There was still sufficient light in the dying sunset for Matt and Alison to identify them.

Aunt Emily was padding backwards and forwards

from Daffodil to Cleopatra, distractedly trying to make up her mind who needed her ministrations more.

Daffodil was leaning against a tree, taking the weight off his injured leg. Aunt Emily fussed around him, sniffing and grunting, until Daffodil finally moved away from the tree, slumped down onto his knees and rolled over onto his side. His leg, Alison noticed, was now completely encased in dried, black mud.

Satisfied that she had got him settled for the night, Aunt Emily stumped off to inspect Cleopatra.

Cleopatra was obviously very uncomfortable. She was standing several metres away from the other elephants. Her head hung low; the tip of her trunk almost touched the ground. She was breathing rapidly and shifting her weight from one foot to the other.

'She's getting near, I'm sure,' Alison said.

'Hm. I suppose all the traumas and the running will have speeded things up for her. I guess we won't have long to wait. The sky's clear. Let's hope for a decent moon. It would be a pity to miss things now.'

'Just look at Emily.'

She had come up behind Cleopatra and was pushing her, trying to make her move back to the rest of the herd. Cleopatra raised her head and bellowed in defiance. Emily ignored her and continued pushing until she had manoeuvred Cleopatra under a tree.

Matt and Alison smiled.

Still not happy with things, Emily stood by her, grunting and grumbling, until Cleopatra finally gave in and did as she was told. With great care she lowered herself to her knees and gently rolled over onto her side.

'No doubt who's in charge, is there? It's like being

in a hospital and watching a bossy midwife ordering a mum-to-be about,' Matt observed.

'I know.'

'So, we might as well settle down ourselves. No doubt there'll be a lot of fuss and discussion when things start to get under way. Why don't we take it in turns to sleep for a while? It'll be a long night otherwise.'

'Good idea.'

'You sleep first then. I'll give you a shout if anything occurs.'

And gradually the shufflings and rumblings from the copse ceased, the soft African night drew in, and they began their vigil.

It was just after 5 a.m. when Cleopatra next moved.

She groaned heavily and rocked herself from side to side until she rolled over onto her stomach. With great difficulty she rose first onto her knees, then heaved herself to her feet. The rest of the herd stirred and grunted sleepily but made no move. Aunt Emily lifted her head, snorted, flapped her ears a couple of times and then laid her head down again.

Cleopatra walked away from the herd, out onto open ground, and began to feed, without enthusiasm, on a small patch of scrub.

Matt nudged Alison awake.

The first glimmerings of dawn were beginning to seep up from the horizon and the trees of the copse were silhouetted black against a silvering landscape. The elephants lay like great grey stones on the ground.

'Come on, wake up,' said Matt. 'She's moving.'

Alison rubbed the sleep from her eyes.

'I see her,' she replied.

She reached into her bag and pulled out her diary and pencil. Squinting at her watch she began her recording.

June 30th.

5.06 a.m.: Cleo. awake. Feeding on . . .

'What are those little thorny bushes called?'

'Balanites.'

. . . balanites.

But that was all for a while. Losing all interest in the meal, Cleopatra stopped chewing and stood, head hanging down, and dozed again.

'What do you think?' Matt asked, after about twenty minutes had gone by. 'Shall we go back up and put the kettle on? I'm cold.'

'So am I,' Alison replied. She pulled the sleeping bag up round her shoulders and snuggled her arms down inside it. 'But I'm not moving. It would be just our luck to have our backs turned at the wrong moment. I'm staying here, however long it takes.'

'OK. I'll slip back up, make us a brew and let Dad know what's happening. I guess he'll want to watch too. Call if anything dramatic happens.'

He rose and padded off up the slope towards the camp.

Ten minutes later he was back with steaming mugs of tea.

'Dad coming?' Alison asked.

'No.'

'No? Why not?'

' "No need", he says. He's seen it all before. Apparently elephant birth is one of the most common sights in the African bush. You've only got to wander about for half an hour and you'll see dozens of elephants giving birth all over the place, every ten minutes.'

'Oh. That's the sort of mood he's in, is it?'

'Hmm. One day perhaps we'll make some sense of him.'

'Never.'

It was half an hour before the next occurrence.

Suddenly Cleopatra lifted her head, flapped her ears back against her shoulders with a sharp, startlingly loud slap, and rumbled.

'Ah,' said Matt. 'That's the "Here I am. Where are you?" call. She's decided she needs some company.'

5.50: Cleo. disturbed. Vocalizes.

The rest of the herd immediately began to take some interest. With a good deal of discussion, head shaking and pushing and shoving, the adults started to rise and prod their young into wakefulness. Soon they were all on their feet and going through the almost human ritual of stretching and yawning and scratching themselves. Daffodil was the last to rise. He stood uncertainly, head turned, sniffing suspiciously at his injured leg. Boxer trotted out to see what Cleopatra wanted but she snorted roughly at him. He swung his right foot backwards and forwards for a time in indecision, then retreated again.

Cleopatra was now beginning to show signs of restlessness and increased discomfort. She began scraping the grass in front of her urgently, as though clearing a space. Now and then she would stop and become very still.

'This is it!' said Alison excitedly. 'This is it. The contractions are starting. Watch her when she stops

125

still like that. You can see her pushing. It's actually happening. And we're going to see it.'

She quickly scribbled the next entry.

6.03: Cleo. in labour. Clearing ground.

Over the next few minutes the elephant became more and more agitated. Just below her tail a bulge began to appear and Cleopatra began to move around in a disturbed and uncertain way. She would take a few steps forward, snort and stamp her feet, and then back up again, suddenly turning around as though trying to see what the annoyance was that was behind her.

6.05: Bulge appearing. Cleo. anxious. Restless.

The other elephants now milled around, aware that an event was taking place but uncertain of their part in it. Aunt Emily walked over to Cleopatra and stood near her, but refrained from interfering.

Breathing shallowly now, Cleopatra lay down on her side and remained in that position for about five minutes.

6.07: Cleo. resting.

When she got up again the bulge was much bigger and much lower down. She backed around in a circle twice, grunting with effort, then, suddenly, without any further pushing or any further drama, she gave birth. Unceremoniously the baby elephant, completely enclosed in its foetal sac, slid out and thudded down on to the ground.

6.14: Calf born.

Alison's hand shook with excitement as she made the entry in the diary.

'Look!' she whispered. 'Just look.'

Cleopatra stayed still and quiet for about a minute. Then she turned and began to inspect the object on the floor, first running the tip of her trunk along it, then gently pushing it with her foot. It did not move. She seemed uncertain what it was or what she was supposed to do with it and began scraping the ground around it with her right foreleg.

6.16: Calf in sac. No movement.

'Matt,' said Alison, becoming alarmed. 'What do you think?'

'I don't know. It's very still, isn't it?'

'Come on. Come on,' Alison whispered in encouragement.

Cleopatra pushed the calf again with her foot and there was a sudden explosion of legs kicking within the sac.

Alison cheered softly.

6.18: Calf alive.

'It won't be for long if she doesn't get it out of that sac soon,' Matt said, noticing what she had written.

Cleopatra reached down, as though she had heard Matt, and started prodding the sac with her tusks. The calf kicked again, more strongly and more urgently.

'I don't know why we're so nervous,' Alison replied. 'Elephants have been having babies without our help for about a million years. I suppose Cleopatra knows perfectly well what's she's doing.'

But help was at hand anyway.

Now that the calf was born a great deal of excitement spread through the rest of the herd. Aunt Emily summoned the other females with her 'Come here' rumble and, with a cacophony of snortings and rumblings and ceremonial stampings, they all crowded around Cleopatra and the new arrival, and joined in helping to remove the sac. Soon Matt and Alison could see the calf clearly, lying on its side, kicking strenuously and waving its trunk in the air. Boxer and one of the other adolescent males wandered over to see what all the excitement was about, but Emily sent them packing again with a loud screech of warning. They slunk back to the trees suitably abashed, and stood peering disconsolately at the events from a distance.

Matt laughed and shook his head.

'Males to the waiting room,' he observed.

6.28: *Calf free. Appears well.*

The immediate problem over, the herd began to disperse again, some wandering back to the trees, some moving into open ground and beginning to feed. None moved far away however, and Matt and Alison noticed that the adult elephants periodically lifted their heads from what they were doing to glance back at the new mother and her baby. Apart from that they left Cleopatra to go on to the next stage herself.

She let her calf rest, standing over it, frequently exploring it with the tip of her trunk. But now she had an air of tension, of anxiety. Her body looked stiff and she constantly lifted her head and looked this way and that as though sensing danger.

Her instincts, her race memory, were telling her that she must get her calf up and onto its feet as quickly as possible.

She left the calf less than five minutes to gather its strength, then she tried to lift it. She placed one huge foot against its stomach, hooked her trunk across its back and tried to roll it gently up onto its feet. The calf protested at first, giving a series of strange, hoarse little cries of protest.

'Poor little thing,' Alison said.

6.33: Cleo. lifting calf.

It took several minutes of pulling and manoeuvring before the calf was finally hauled to its feet.

Instantly it collapsed, but this time lay upright, its back legs bent, its front legs straight out. Cleopatra stood back and left it to recover. After another couple of minutes its own survival instincts came into play and it hauled itself laboriously to its feet by itself.

6.41: Calf stands.

It immediately fell down again with a crash.

. . . and falls.

Cleopatra stepped forward and draped her trunk over it to reassure it. After a few seconds it stood again, wobbled and fell again. Finally, after five minutes of practice, the calf stood and remained standing.

'Oh, look at him,' Alison gasped. 'He's beautiful.'

The baby stood, swaying slightly as he explored his new world with his trunk. A tuft of black hair on his forehead gave him a comic, clown-like appearance, a likeness accentuated by blood-red eyes and bright pink ears that seemed far too large for his body.

'Beautiful, eh?' said Matt. 'I suppose he is to a mother elephant.'

'He is to me, and no funny remarks. He's a perfect miniature. He's lovely.'

'Yes.'

Eventually the swaying turned into a lurch which became the first tentative step. The calf looked surprised that it had moved. Then, experimentally, it took another step, and another.

Finally Cleopatra began to walk away and the calf, unsteadily and uncertainly, followed.

The matriarch, Queen Victoria, had seemed to

take little interest in the proceedings up to now. But she had been watching nevertheless, for as soon as she saw that the calf was able to follow its mother she started to rumble her instructions to the herd. The elephants began to assemble from their different points in the copse. When they were all together again, Victoria gave her 'Let's go' rumble and they began to move away. The older adult elephants surrounded Cleopatra and her calf; the adolescents, excited by the unusual activity, dashed hither and thither on the outskirts of the group, trying to get a view of the new member of their family; the young took up their positions by their mothers. Daffodil, limping, joined Aunt Emily at the rear of the group.

Finally, just less than an hour after the birth, the herd left, heading north.

6.59: Calf walking steadily. Herd departs.

'That's it, then,' said Alison. She stood up to watch them depart.

She glanced down at the page of her diary.

'Twelve lines,' she said. 'It looks so ordinary. Such a great event reduced to so few words. It was pointless really.'

She threw the diary onto the ground.

'It's not the words, it's the pictures in your head that they'll bring back. In fifty years' time you'll find that diary stuffed in the bottom of a box, long forgotten, and you'll remember all this.'

'I won't need a diary. I'll never forget.'

'Come on,' said Matt, gathering up the sleeping bags. 'It's all over for the moment. Let's go and get some breakfast and report to Dad. Then we'll get on the move. We're going back to the Research Institute at Seronera this morning. We'll catch up with the herd again tomorrow. They won't go far today. Daffodil won't be able to walk too well for a day or two and the calf will need to rest often.'

'Right.'

They started to climb back up the hillside to the camp.

Just before they crested the rise, Alison stopped suddenly.

'Oh,' she said.

'What? What's the matter?' Matt turned and looked at her curiously. Alison had a strange, puzzled look on her face.

'Alison?' Matt asked when she did not reply. 'What's the matter?'

'I don't know. I suddenly went all cold and shivery. Just for a second.' She smiled uncertainly. 'Somebody walked over my grave.'

'Just reaction, I suppose. It's been an emotional twenty-four hours. Come on. Coffee will put you right.'

Matt turned and continued on up to the camp.

Alison hesitated slightly before following.

She turned and looked back at the herd. Even moving so slowly they had covered a surprising distance, and she was unable to see the calf now.

She watched them gliding away from her. The rising sun was pulling a faint mist up from the ground and the elephants' shapes were softened by it. Distance was giving them a strange, surreal aspect. A phantom herd whispering silently away across a ghost-white plain.

Alison felt a strange sense of anticlimax. It had all been over so soon.

And now they were leaving.

A powerful sense of loss coursed through her, though instantly she recognized that it was foolish to feel like that. She had no place in the lives of the elephants and never could have.

But somehow, nevertheless, she felt they were taking with them something which belonged to her.

She sighed and lifted her eyes to scan the vast tract of land between the herd and the mist-shrouded strangeness of distant Gelai Peak.

She shivered again.

Far, far away, a tiny black shape, back-lit by the pale yellow light of the sunrise, stood motionless on the horizon.

Though distance diminished him, reduced his great frame to a dot in an immense, soundless landscape. Alison knew instantly who he was.

And knew also that he had been there all night. Watching, listening, guarding.

Knowing.

Once again she felt the great sadness which had so hurt her heart. Only this time she knew why – knew what she had seen in his eyes, what had been there behind the wonderment.

Loneliness was what she had seen.

Hiding within this creature's great body, masked by his great power, was the vulnerability of the lonely.

His solitary figure, miniaturized by distance, shrunk to insignificance by the immensity of Africa, was a distillation of what his eyes had revealed.

A metaphor of tiny lives played out in an ancient and uncaring land. Of beginnings and endings. Of lonely life and lonelier death.

Alison looked back at the herd. In her mind she could see the little calf wobbling precariously along behind his mother.

'Have a long, good life,' she whispered.

When she raised her eyes back to the horizon the bull was gone.

But she whispered to him too.

'I know you're there. Watch over him.'

SEVENTEEN

*'Turning and turning in the widening gyre
The falcon cannot hear the falconer;
Things fall apart; the centre cannot hold.'*

W.B. Yeats, *The Second Coming*, 1921

Benny finished transferring petrol from the jerrycans into the main tanks, then climbed into the driving seat, turned the ignition key and started the Land Rover.

'OK,' he grinned. 'We go.'

It was just after seven in the morning and heat was beginning to threaten the day.

'Well, I'm really sorry to hear that,' said Hyram, wiping his forehead and looking around the *manyatta* with distaste. 'But at least I've leaving standing up. That's something. I expected to be going out of here feet first.'

Benny grinned more widely.

'There was no danger, *bwana*.'

'No. Course not.' Hyram was not convinced. 'Real sweethearts, these guys.'

Benny chuckled and engaged gear. He steered out

through the gap in the thorn fence, swung the Land Rover round until the compass on the dashboard read south-west and began to head away.

Mike was slumped in the passenger seat, peering closely at a map.

'And I ain't pleased with you either,' Hyram added, without looking at him.

'I know, Hyram. And I'm really upset about that. Devastated. I haven't slept a wink all night for the worry.'

'Schmuck.'

'Hyram, what does it take to satisfy you? We've got an agreement from the Maasai. I thought you'd be happy. That's what we came for, isn't it?'

'Yeah. That's what we came for. It's how you got there I don't like.'

'I told you last night to get things in perspective. For all you know this bull, Papa Tembo, could be near the end of his life anyway. Isn't it just common sense to sacrifice him if we can track down van der Wel and have him arrested?'

Hyram was silent.

'Well, isn't it?' Mike persisted.

'Schmuck,' said Hyram.

Mike sighed.

'Anyway,' Hyram added a few moments later, brightening. 'It's all academic. With your record he'll die of old age before you find him. Probably we all will.'

Mike irritably returned to studying the map.

'I've made the bargain. I'm going to keep it,' he said. 'He was heading south-west yesterday. I intend to find him.'

'You might not need to, *bwana*,' Benny interrupted quietly, smiling to himself.

'What?'

'While you and the headman were playing power games, I was persuading the cousin of the friend of my friend in another way.'

'What do you mean "persuading"? What other way?'

'Your whisky bottle's empty.'

There was a short silence.

'I love this guy,' chortled Hyram, finally. 'I love him.'

'He enjoyed the whisky,' said Benny. 'He was very grateful.'

Mike stared stonily ahead through the windscreen.

'Was he?' he snarled, through clenched teeth. 'Considering that was probably the last bottle of whisky in Tanzania, I should hope he was.'

'And . . . ?' asked Hyram.

'And we made a bargain of our own. He thinks he knows where van der Wel has his base. He says that, years ago, when he was young, when he was a *morani*, he followed a lion round the base of Ol Doinyo Lengai, in that hollow between Lengai and Ngorongoro where nothing lives. He says he saw a truck drive into there and vanish.'

'I don't suppose it occurred to you that, so long as you were happy to feed him whisky, he'd be happy to tell you anything he thought you might want to know, true or not?'

'Aw, come on,' said Hyram. 'That's just sour grapes. You're peeved because Benny's cracked it when you didn't.'

'Not at all. He'll be laughing at us, knowing he's sent us off on a wild-goose chase. Except he hasn't, because we're not following it up. We'll stick to my plan.'

'May I remind you,' said Hyram, slowly and deliberately, 'as indeed I had to remind you last time I was here and hired you to drive me around this godforsaken country, that I am the man with the wallet. That is my goddamn petrol that's going through that goddamn engine in front of you, so I call the goddamn shots. Right?'

'Now listen to me!' Mike snapped, spinning round angrily to face Hyram. 'You might be paying but—'

'He's there!' Benny cut in suddenly. 'Look ahead.'

They looked through the windscreen.

In the distance a lone Maasai stood, on one leg, like a long, scarlet bird, waiting under a tree.

'He's coming with us. He's going to show us where he saw the truck.'

'Oh,' said Mike, temporarily deflated. 'Oh well, I suppose it's worth a try.'

Hyram grinned and fell silent.

Benny stared straight ahead, his face an expressionless mask. A grin from him, he decided, would be one step too far.

Laurens van der Wel finished loading the jerrycans of water into the cab of the Bedford.

This was one job he always did for himself. Filled the bottles himself, padlocked the tops himself and locked them in the truck's cab himself. No one had ever been trusted with this task. If things go wrong out there in the bush, in the huge, lonely wastelands, water is life. Food you can find, or if you can't, you can survive for many days without it. But twenty-four hours without water and the merciless heat of Africa will desiccate your brain. You tire. You hallucinate. You stumble, eagerly, towards things that are not there. And then you die.

And these men, they hated him. He knew that.

In his presence they fawned and flattered and ingratiated themselves. But he wasn't fooled. When his back was turned their servility faded instantly and revealed their bitter loathing.

He could feel their eyes sometimes on his back, feel the malevolence of their gaze. Any one of them would kill him if they got the opportunity. But they would never face him, never challenge him openly. They were too afraid of him for that. They would do it stealthily, secretly.

And what easier way than by poisoning the water?

He checked the padlocks again.

He turned and looked at the men. His lip curled, contemptuously. Even now they were up to something, grouped together, huddled in some sort of conspiracy, muttering inaudibly.

'Right!' he snarled, clapping his hands together. 'Break it up and let's get on our way. Enough talk.'

The men stayed where they were.

Van der Wel eyed them suspiciously for a moment or two, trying to gauge their mood. Then he stepped forward, his fingers caressing the shaft of the *sjambok*.

'I said *move!*'

The Mchawi detached himself from the group.

'*Bwana*,' he said. He was hesitant, nervous. 'Today we should not hunt.'

The men behind him murmured in agreement.

Van der Wel's eyes registered surprise, but almost instantly hardened.

'What?' he hissed, quietly.

'The signs, *bwana* . . .' the Mchawi explained. His voice quavered a little as he spoke. 'The signs are not good. The men are unhappy.'

'Are they?' Laurens van der Wel's voice was heavy with sarcasm. 'Well, well. Unhappy, are they?'

He took another step forward and slipped the *sjambok* out of his belt.

'Perhaps they would wish to be more unhappy. Or perhaps you could persuade them that I do not pay them to be happy. Perhaps you could persuade them that I pay them to do as they are told, which is precisely . . .'

The *sjambok* hissed through the air and bit deeply into the Mchawi's shoulder.

'. . . what I pay you for.'

The man staggered back and raised his arms in front of his face to protect himself.

There was a gasp of anger from the group.

Two of the men stepped forward but stopped again immediately as van der Wel's hand went to the revolver at his belt. They shrank back again as he flipped open the clasp of the holster.

'*Bwana*,' the Mchawi persisted, 'the hunt will fail. The Ritual tells us so. This morning the grain is scattered. It is bad. The hunt will fail. There will be danger.'

Van der Wel pulled out the revolver and pointed it directly at the Mchawi's forehead.

'Ritual?' he snarled, his voice acid with contempt. 'Ritual? I'll tell you what is the ritual. This!'

He pressed the muzzle of the gun against the Mchawi's forehead.

'The gun. And the bullet. And the finger on the trigger. This is the ritual. This is what makes the difference. This is what the elephant knows. Nothing else.'

The Mchawi had frozen with fear. He stared past the gun into van der Wel's cold eyes.

'So choose,' van der Wel whispered, drawing the words out slowly so that he hissed like a snake about to strike. '*Choose!*'

There was a long pause as they confronted each other. But in the end there was no choice and the Mchawi knew it. Van der Wel, balanced precariously and permanently on the edge of terrible violence, would have no qualms whatsoever about shooting him.

Eventually the Mchawi turned slowly away and walked back to his men.

'We go,' he said, shrugging helplessly.

There was much shaking of heads and muttering, but the group, recognizing defeat, began to disperse. Slowly, making their reluctance and anger obvious, they shuffled over to the Bedford truck and the Land Rovers and climbed in.

Only when they were all in their vehicles did Laurens van der Wel put his revolver back into its holster.

Then he hauled himself up into the cab of the Bedford, turned the ignition key and fired the big diesel engine into life. He allowed a minute for the engine to settle itself into a steady, reassuring thud, then he reversed, swung the machine round and began to grind slowly out of the compound.

The Land Rovers fell into convoy behind him.

*

The men gradually quietened as the vehicles began to negotiate the deep gullies, passages and clefts which were their exit route. But, though quiet, they were rebelliously unhappy.

For the Ritual could not be flouted; the spirits could not be ignored.

Laurens van der Wel was right. The guns *were* all-powerful; twentieth-century artefacts which paid no heed to the ancient Ritual.

But in Africa the twentieth century has to live side by side with older things.

Today, in this hunt, the elephants might die. But without the spirits' agreement there would be no protection for the men.

And not only that. There would be revenge for disobedience, revenge for not heeding the signs. Perhaps not this time. Perhaps not even next. But eventually it would come.

Out of nowhere a tusk would pierce your body, a foot would crush your skull like an eggshell, a powerful trunk would pluck you from your feet like a feather and smash you against a tree.

These things would happen, as surely as night followed day.

Disgustedly, the Mchawi reached into his bag and pulled out the sacking bundle which contained the elephant heart.

It was useless now. Their spells were ruined.

Angrily he hurled it out of the back of the truck.

Matt finished rolling up the tents, stuffed them into their bags and threw them into the back of the Land Rover. Then he walked a few metres away from the campsite and dumped the remaining contents of the cold-box at the foot of a tree.

'That's it,' he announced. 'That's all the old bacon and meat got rid of. Somebody will come along and enjoy it later.'

' "Never throw food away, no matter how rotten",' Alison said in a sing-song voice. 'Isn't that what you always used to drill into me? "You never know when you'll need it." '

'Hmm. I know. But we'll be in Seronera in a few hours. And frankly, if we get stuck, I'd rather die of starvation than eat that bacon. It's been there so long it's evolved. It's grown legs. It was walking around in the bottom of the box.'

John Blake was sitting on a rock, writing up his journal.

'I'll just do this,' he said, 'and then we'll get on our way.'

He had started a new page for the calf.

5/13. Male. b. 28 June of cow 5/12, age 24.

Then he had copied Alison's entries.

'Did you see whether it suckled at all?' he asked.

Alison was sitting near him, reading her own diary and reliving the event.

'No. They all left as soon as he was able to walk. How soon will he need to feed?'

'Within a few hours really. Especially if they make it walk far. It will soon become weak.'

'Well, we'd better get on our way then. The sooner we get to Seronera, the sooner we're back to keep an eye on things. It's a nuisance having to go at all.'

John Blake smiled gently at his daughter's concern.

'That's all you can do. Watch. You know that, don't you?'

Alison stared at him, puzzled.

'Yes, of course I know. What do you mean?'

'I mean you couldn't interfere, whatever happens.'

'I know that. Why are you saying this? Why would I want to interfere?'

'This isn't her first calf.'

There was a long pause while Alison assimilated the information.

'Oh. I didn't know.'

'I didn't tell you.'

Alison was quiet again for a moment. She closed her book and stared out into the distance, in the direction the herd had taken.

'I have to give you some advice,' John Blake said. 'You won't like it. And this isn't the scientist speaking, it's the dad. You're allowing yourself to become too involved.'

'That sounds like the scientist to me.'

'No, it's nothing to do with that. It's to do with emotions. This is a herd of wild animals surviving in a very difficult place. Our job is to find out how they do that. That's the scientific bit. Allow yourself to become too involved with their lives and the science suffers, certainly. But that's not what's bothering me.'

'What then?'

'You'll suffer too. You're already suffering. You're letting their lives get inside you. That's a big mistake.'

Alison was silent for a long time.

'What happened to the other calf?' she asked, finally.

'It was during the drought, three years ago. The

calf was undernourished in the womb. It was tiny when it was born. And Cleopatra had no milk anyway, so it only survived a few hours.'

'Oh.'

'And that sums up what I'm trying to say. If you allow their lives inside you, you have to have room also for their deaths. And in most of us there isn't room. Think of it like being a doctor or a nurse. You can't spread your heart wide enough to cover all your patients' problems. You'd go mad if you tried. It's the same here. Close your heart. Or you can be very sure that one day they'll break it for you.'

A picture of the tiny, wobbly calf, so new, so fragile, came into Alison's mind again.

'So, what are his chances?' she asked after a long pause.

'The scientific facts?'

'The scientific facts.'

'In good times 90 per cent of calves might survive. In bad 20 per cent. But there's no rule. Tell yourself that this calf has a 50/50 chance. Call him 5/13 and see him as a unit in the herd. Nothing more than that. That way you'll protect yourself from him.'

'Is that how you see him?'

'That's exactly how I see him. A unit. Nothing more. Now let's get on our way. And think about what I've said.'

John Blake stood and began to busy himself collecting his journal and papers, stuffing them untidily into his briefcase.

He paused for a second to rub his eyes.

Noticing that Alison was still watching him he turned away.

'And douse that damn fire properly, will you, Matt,' he snapped as he stumped off towards the Land Rover. The blasted smoke's getting in my eyes.'

Yes, Dad,' Matt replied, mildly.

He winked at Alison.

Alison nodded gently back to him.

'Yes, Dad,' she said, softly.

Fifteen minutes later the Blakes' Land Rover bumped slowly down the hillside and out onto open ground. Matt pointed the vehicle due west.

'Two or three hours and we'll join the Lobo-Seronera road. After that it's plain sailing,' he announced.

Thirty kilometres to the south-west the engine of the Bedford roared as Laurens van der Wel crashed and bounced the four-tonne truck through the black sand-troughs at the foot of Ol Doinyo Lengai.

He barely saw the land he was negotiating.

Ahead of him, through the windscreen, looming massively in his mind's eye, was only one thing. The figure of the great bull elephant which had dominated his life.

'Perhaps today,' he said to himself. 'Perhaps today.'

Thirty kilometres to the north Benny hummed cheerfully as he bowled the Land Rover along on open grassland.

Mike Taylor snoozed in the passenger seat.

Hyram T. Johnson sweated. He wrinkled his nose as the heat of the day built and the animal fat on the skin of the stone-silent Maasai sitting next to him turned rancid.

'Jeez,' he commented, quietly.

Beyond the horizon Papa Tembo trod out his day.
He was far away.
Much too far away to see or hear the herd.
But he could see and hear them nevertheless.

And the herd fed quietly.
Unsuspectingly.
At peace in the soft morning sun.

EIGHTEEN

*'Somewhere the sky touches the earth
and the name of that place is The End.'*

Kamba saying

'There's this godforsaken place in South Dakota, or some goddamn spot like that. I went there once. Jeez.'

Hyram shuddered with horror at the memory.

'They call it "The Badlands". But I'll tell you, it ain't got nothing on this.'

Mike and Hyram stood, sweating heavily in the noon sun, and staring, bleakly, at the approach to the lower slopes of Ol Doinyo Lengai.

Above them towered a grid of steep ridges, jagged like blackened teeth. Separating them from the ridges were deep gullies. Beyond them rose only desolate, barren lava flow.

Their footsteps resounded as they moved, for the mountain is hollow.

To add to their dismay, the Land Rover was stuck, sunk up to its axles in the river of black sand which wound around the base of the volcano.

Benny was digging irritably around the wheels, grumbling vehemently under his breath in Swahili.

'What's he saying?' Hyram asked.

'Something about the mental capacities and intelligence of the Maasai, as far as I can understand it,' Mike replied, grinning. 'At least that's the bit I can tell you. The rest of what he's saying isn't for the ears of someone of delicate nature like you, Hyram.'

'I'm beginning to think you might be right, *bwana*,' Benny snapped. 'I'm not sure this man knows anything at all.'

Mike smiled his 'I told you so' smile but said nothing.

The Maasai tribesman was stalking up and down purposefully, some distance away from them. Now and then he would stop and stare hard at the slopes of the mountain, but each time would shake his head and move on. His long figure moved quickly but gracefully, the red robe billowing out behind him in the hot, sulphurous down-draughts which swept continuously down the lava flows.

'You said nothing lived here, Benny. I think you're right. Not even a goddamn loony like van der Wel would live here. Would he?'

'I'll reserve judgement for a bit longer,' Mike replied. 'We might as well give this man the benefit of the doubt. We can't go anywhere anyway.'

He turned, walked over to the Land Rover and dragged a heavy, long-handled axe out of the back.

'Here,' he said to Hyram. 'Do something useful. Go and chop a few branches off that tree. We can shove them under the wheels. See if we can get some grip.'

A gnarled, twisted acacia had somehow struggled into life in the lunar ash about twenty metres from where they stood, but its existence had been short and brutal and it was long since dead.

'And what about you?' grumbled Hyram as he set off. 'What's the Great White Hunter's contribution going to be?'

Mike ignored him, returned to the Land Rover and got his binoculars. He climbed up onto the vehicle's roof and scanned the slopes carefully.

Benny finished digging at the front wheels and started on the back.

'Another ten minutes or so, *bwana*, and we'll try again.'

The Maasai disappeared into a deep *donga*, but in the heavy silence they could hear his feet scuffing rapidly through the dust.

Hyram reached the tree and began to whack at it in a perfunctory, indifferent fashion. Gradually a branch or two began to accumulate on the ground.

He wrinkled his nostrils periodically, without for a time giving it any thought. The air was heavy with the stench of sulphur. But something else was there too. Something mingling with the sulphur. Something which bothered him subconsciously and took time to rise to the surface of his brain.

Eventually it registered.

'Jeez,' he said, nosing the air appraisingly. Then he shouted.

'Taylor!'

'What?'

'There might be nothing lives here now, but something sure did. 'Cos it's dead.'

'What're you talking about?'

'There's something dead around here, stinking to high heaven.'

'A tourist perhaps,' Mike muttered under his breath. 'Or is that too much to hope for?'

'So what?' he called back.

'Schmuck!' said Hyram.

He threw the axe down and started to investigate.

'So it might be important, that's what. It might be a goddamn elephant or something, that's what. It might give us a goddamn clue, that's what.'

He walked on past the tree, sniffing the air as he went.

The ground rose up off the black sand onto a lava slope. He followed the rise of the slope, heading up towards a ridge.

The smell got heavier and more distasteful as he progressed upwards until he was forced to hold a handkerchief in front of his nose and breathe through his mouth. Cresting the ridge, he found the ground cut away, precipitously, into a gully cut deep in the lava.

The stench was overpowering as Hyram slid down the steep side of the *donga*.

It did not take him long to trace its source.

'Jeez!' he said, regarding the object on the ground with revulsion.

Feeling sick, he tentatively pushed the lump of bloodstained stacking with his foot. He retched violently as its rotting fabric tore under his boot and allowed the putrescent, maggot-boiling lump of meat to roll sickeningly out onto the dusty ground.

'Jeeeez . . .' he moaned again, with a long exhalation of breath. 'What . . . in God's name . . . is that?'

So revolted was he, so disgusted at the unspeakable vileness of this crawling, filthy mass, that instinct made him lash out at the thing, to get it away from him.

His right foot surged forward, kicking the foulness away.

It was a heavy, well-aimed kick. The bundle rose up into the air and sailed in an arc across the *donga*.

Hyram followed it with his eyes.

It fell with a wet, stomach-turning thump into the dust, several metres away.

'Good goddamn riddance, whatever you were,' he said.

And was about to turn away and go back.

But didn't.

Something stopped him.

He screwed up his eyes against the glare of the sun and looked hard at the black sand where the thing had fallen.

There was something there, something he couldn't quite make out.

Overcoming his reluctance to go near the vile thing again, he took a few steps across to where it lay.

A wide grin spread across his face.

'Taylor!' he called.

'What?'

'Keep that self-satisfied smirk on your face, will you,' Hyram chuckled happily. 'Because I want to watch as I wipe it off.'

*

The Maasai was walking away, heading back to the *manyatta*, his job done.

'Will he be all right?' Hyram asked, watching him float away into seemingly endless plain. 'It's a hell of a way back.'

'He'll be all right,' Benny replied. 'Fifty kilometres or so. Nothing to a Maasai. They can run all day. And all night. And all the next day if they want to. He'll be home before dark.'

'I hope you took back those things you were saying about him. He was right after all.'

'Yes.'

'Huh!' snorted Mike. 'Approximately right, at most. It was pure luck, admit it. He could have walked up and down from now till kingdom come. If you hadn't found the tyre track we'd be no nearer. That was luck.'

'Ready now, *bwana*,' Benny announced, as he climbed into the driver's seat and started the engine. 'I'll try reversing out.'

Mike and Hyram took up position at the front of the vehicle and pushed.

Benny engaged low-ratio gears and, with his foot barely touching the accelerator, allowed the vehicle to inch slowly backwards. It slipped a couple of times, throwing up black dust, but gradually it crept up out of the ruts and lurched across the sand river until it reached firmer ground.

Benny stopped and allowed the engine to tick over.

'Right,' said Hyram, as he and Mike climbed in. 'Let's see what we find.'

Slowly, Benny crept along the edge of the sand

154

river and manoeuvred the Land Rover round into the gully.

'Over there, just beside that rock.'

Hyram pointed along the gully to where he had found the tyre track and Benny pulled up beside it.

'Bedford four-tonner,' he announced.

'I don't care what it is. Where's it come from? That's what interests me. Head up here.'

Benny engaged gear again and the Land Rover ground slowly along the floor of the gully. They found that the crevasse wound itself into the mountainside, rising gently up the lava-slope. And, as they proceeded into it, the sides gradually became steeper, restricting their vision, eventually, to a narrow corridor of black rock.

Then, turning a sharp corner, they found that the ground began to slope away downwards in front of them.

Benny halted briefly and engaged low-ratio again. He put the vehicle into second gear and allowed the engine to take them down the gradient at its own pace.

It was a long, slow drop.

Light began to fade as they descended, until eventually it was so dim that Benny was forced to put the Land Rover's headlamps on. They were entering a deep ravine in the side of the mountain, a great gash sinking into the volcano's flank.

Still they descended, grinding slowly down, down.

Hyram stuck his head out of the window and looked up. The black walls of the gully now rose sheer, towering thirty metres or more to culminate in a narrow crack of light high above them.

The air was stiflingly hot and sulphurous.

'Jeez!' he remarked, gasping for air.

'Another wild-goose chase,' moaned Mike, staring irritably ahead. 'This is hardly wide enough for the Land Rover, let alone a Bedford. He didn't come this way.'

'You seen any other way he could have come? We followed the goddamn tracks into here. Where else could he have come from, if not here?'

'I know what's happened,' said Mike. 'We're all dead. That's what's happened. We've had an accident but don't know it. We were all killed and we're on our way to hell.'

'Aw, shut up,' Hyram replied. 'Defeatist.'

The ground began to level.

Benny negotiated the Land Rover around a sharp, right-hand turn.

Hyram drew in his breath.

'Take a look at that, will you?'

The gully walls had now closed completely over them and they were in total blackness. They were entering a long, natural corridor leading ever deeper into the mountain.

Benny stopped the Land Rover, unwilling to proceed into the yawning blackness.

The powerful headlights shone eerily ahead of them but failed to reveal the end of the corridor, so long was it.

'Keep going,' Hyram ordered.

Benny let in the clutch and the vehicle began to edge slowly into the darkness. The soft throb of the engine echoed back, amplified, from the smooth black walls.

Mike found that he was gripping the dashboard

tightly. Cold beads of sweat started to trickle down into his eyes.

'I don't know whether van der Wel's a loony or not,' he muttered, 'but the day I agreed to this barmy idea must have put me firmly in that category too.'

He was disturbed to discover that his voice sounded strange, constricted.

He coughed, nervously, as though to clear his throat.

'Something wrong?' asked Hyram cruelly, noticing the tension.

'No,' Mike replied.

But he said it too loudly, too emphatically. He was experiencing the terrors of claustrophobia, but was damned if he was going to show it. Damned if he was going to let Hyram know that, although the mountain had been here for a thousand million years, it was going to choose this precise moment in the history of the planet to collapse in upon itself, trapping them for eternity.

He gripped the dashboard tighter and breathed deeply and slowly.

'Get a grip,' he whispered in his mind.

He was just on the point of panic, just on the point of hurling the Land Rover door open and leaping out, when a faint, white glow began to appear ahead of them.

'Aha!' said Hyram softly. 'Light at the end of the tunnel. In more senses than one, I hope. Go steady now.'

Mike fixed his eyes firmly and gratefully on the light.

They emerged through the tunnel's end and out into the light.

Immediately Benny braked, hard. Then he clunked the gear lever into reverse, pulled the vehicle back into the tunnel again and switched off the engine.

There was a moment's silence.

It was broken by Mike.

'Before you say anything, Hyram,' he said, very quietly, 'I'm already doing it.'

'Doing what?'

'Eating my words.'

They climbed out of the Land Rover and walked out of the tunnel.

'Jeez!' said Hyram. 'Just take a look at that, will you. No wonder this guy's never been caught.'

They stared down at the collection of buildings packed tightly into the depression below them, and marvelled at the nature of the place.

It was an almost completely circular volcanic crater in miniature, sucked in aeons ago in a long-forgotten eruption. A small pockmark only, less than half a kilometre across, barely scarring Lengai's side. Completely enclosed by jagged walls of ancient lava, from even a short distance it would have been invisible to the uninquisitive eye, blending imperceptibly into the face of the mountain.

Just an accident of geology, a freak ancient bubble of liquid earth, caught and frozen by time. But a freak of such perfection that it could have been made for its present purpose.

A perfect place to hide.

'Any sign of life?' Hyram asked.

'I don't see any. Looks deserted. No vehicles either.'

'So what are we waiting for?'

Hyram began to stamp off down the slope, heading towards the huts.

Benny had already anticipated this next move.

'Here, *bwana*,' he called after him. 'Take this.'

He caught up with Hyram and handed him the Brno .22 semi-automatic rifle. To Mike he passed the immensely powerful .416.

'They may have left a guard,' Benny explained.

'Slow down a bit, Hyram, will you?' Mike ordered. 'In spite of all I say, I don't want you to get shot. Not least because I'd have to deal with all the mess. Let's exercise a bit of caution.'

'OK.'

They spread well out, then slowly and vigilantly crept down the slope, through the open barbed-wire gate and into the compound.

It was, as they had thought, deserted.

Hyram stood for a long moment, looking around.

'Swap guns for a minute, Taylor?' he asked, finally.

'Can you handle this? Big enough to knock the engine out of a car, this one.'

'Jeez,' Hyram said, shaking his head at Benny. 'He asks me if I can handle it. I was handling bigger guns than this in the Korean war when I was eighteen. When he was still in nappies.'

He held out the .22 to Mike.

'Just pass that here, will you, then we'll see who can handle it.'

Taking the .416 he turned, walked across to the nearest of the huts and inspected the heavily padlocked door.

'So,' he muttered darkly, 'let's see what we've got here.'

Then he raised the gun to waist height and, without ceremony, blasted the door clean off its hinges.

NINETEEN

'The death of an important animal such as the matriarch has a profound effect on the family. There can be total disintegration for a long period afterward, with some families never resuming their former cohesiveness.'

Cynthia Moss, *Elephant Memories*, 1988

Laurens van der Wel sat with his back against a rock, scanning the plain through binoculars. His men lounged silently against the Land Rovers or lay stretched out on the ground, waiting. The sun was moving past its zenith. The men fidgeted in the searing heat and flailed miserably at the tsetse flies droning around their heads.

They had drawn the vehicles up to the top of a low hill from where they had a complete panorama of the landscape.

They had spotted the herd almost immediately, but, inexplicably, van der Wel had not ordered them to move towards it. Instead he had sat in the same position, just as he was now, for more than an hour. In his normal contemptuous manner he had not told them what he was thinking and they, demoralized and quietly surly, did not bother to ask.

He was not watching the herd anyway.

He was sectioning the plain, inch by inch, examining every tree, every rock, every depression in the ground, every shadow.

Meticulously, obsessively searching.

Finally he gave up, swung the binoculars back on to the grazing herd and began to explore the area immediately around it.

The elephants were grouped in the shade of a clump of trees, hiding from the sun. Unless anything disturbed them they would, he knew, stay there now until mid-afternoon, until the searing heat began to abate.

So there was no hurry about what he was planning.

In ordinary circumstances the job would have been straightforward and easy. Simply send the vehicles out quietly to the points of the compass then, on a signal, approach the elephants at speed from all four sides.

Confuse them, separate them and despatch them as quickly as possible. That was the usual plan. Get them running in all directions, panicked, and just pick them off, one by one. Simple. A turkey shoot. They'd done it a hundred times.

But today was not ordinary.

Papa Tembo was out there somewhere. And van der Wel knew it.

Though the binoculars had not revealed him, he was there nevertheless, just beyond vision. His presence *felt*.

So today the plan would be different.

Van der Wel continued searching the area until he found what he was looking for. Then he called the Mchawi over.

'To the left of the herd,' he said, handing the man the binoculars. 'About a kilometre away from them.'

The Mchawi raised the glasses to his eyes.

'Yes, *bwana*?'

'The small hill there.'

The binoculars swept across the plain until they came to rest on the hill.

'I know it, *bwana*.'

'At the end. The rocks.'

The Mchawi scanned along the hill. In length it was perhaps half a kilometre, but nowhere was it more than twenty metres high. Undistinguished, apart from the strange conformation which gave it its name, it sat in isolation on the plain. Here and there the stone pushed its way through the grass like jutting bones, so that the shape of the hill was drawn in outline by a jagged grey line at the top of the steep, grassed slopes. One of many ancient volcanic bubbles in this strange terrain, the rock had been pushed up to form a circle, a deep pockmark, creating within its walls a huge natural enclosure. At the mound's southern end the rock formed into two long, low spurs which swept out from the body of the hill. From a distance they resembled the great, curving horns of the bony, Maasai cattle. At their points the spurs almost met, leaving only a narrow gap for entry.

'The Maasai call it Cattle Rock,' the Mchawi said.

'I want the herd in there. All of them. In that amphitheatre.'

The Mchawi was mystified.

He studied the area, glancing sideways at van der Wel. The man's face was hard.

The Mchawi shrugged. He wasn't going to query him.

It didn't matter anyway. What was it to him, or to his men, what scheme van der Wel had in mind? Their job was simple. *Do what you're paid to do.* That was what the *bwana* had said. So that was what they would do.

But only so far, he thought. *For a man who despises the Ritual, only so far.*

'Yes, *bwana*,' he said.

'So,' said van der Wel. 'Get your men on their feet. This is how we will proceed.'

Queen Victoria was the first to hear the softly throbbing engines. At first she took little notice. She had long ago become used to this sound and to the sight of the things that made it. Provided they didn't come too close she would tolerate them, just as she would tolerate most things which passed by daily on the plains. Lion, wildebeest or Land Rover, it was all the same to her. If they posed no threat they could go about their business unchallenged.

But never did the sound go unnoticed, never was it dismissed without first being assessed, never was its potential for danger underestimated.

So she listened again, and began to give it more attention.

For this was a different sound.

She rumbled a warning to the dozing herd. They stirred and rumbled in reply as Victoria stamped out of the trees, flapping her ears. As soon as she was out onto open ground she stopped and concentrated, trying to identify from where the sound came.

The other elephants began to move uncertainly, edging this way and that, organizing the young to be in readiness, waiting for the matriarch to give them further instructions.

Cleopatra pushed her sleeping calf until he woke; then pushed him more until he stood, confused, beside her legs.

But the instructions did not come.

Victoria turned her head quizzically from side to side. She took a few steps forward in one direction, then stopped and listened; lurched briefly in another direction; stopped and listened; backed up a little; and eventually stood still again.

Confused, indecisive, she swung one of her front legs backwards and forwards.

She swept her great head slowly in an arc from left to right.

And still could not place the sound.

It seemed as though it came from everywhere. The whole plain seemed to pulsate with the noise.

She peered carefully out into the distance, anxious that her eyes should reveal what her ears could not. Her brain sifted the information before her; sorted the images of trees and rocks and hills and plain and the things that moved upon and between them; noted the shadowed humps rising from the foot of a sweeping thorn tree and registered them as lions; passed over the herds of gazelle and zebra and wildebeest as irrelevant, except to notice that they were disturbed, restless, raising their heads and prancing brief dances of alarm. Apprehensively she wondered why dark clouds of birds spiralled up from the horizon.

Gradually but inexorably, as she watched, the restlessness grew and took form.

Animals were summoned back from their grazing by warning bellows and whinnies; calves and cubs were ordered to return from play by peremptory roars and grunts.

Everything began to move back to its own kind. Wildebeest, stretched out in long feeding-skeins, began to wind themselves back into the herd. They swiftly congealed themselves into a heavy, dark mass and then, as though on a single given command, flowed away, like liquid, across the plain. Zebra skittered away in wispy, mirage-shimmering clouds of black and white, and gazelles hurled themselves tangentially into the air, literally *bouncing* their way out of danger. Victoria felt the thunder of tens of thousands of panicked hooves vibrating up through the soles of her feet, and her anxiety increased.

She stamped forward a few paces in mock attack, thudding her feet hard into the earth, sending her warning through the ground. But it was a futile gesture, for she could see nothing yet to attack.

Soon clouds of dust, kicked up by the fleeing, frightened feet, obscured the horizon.

She stood, blindly watching. Waiting.

And eventually the danger began to emerge. Rolling slowly out of the dust cloud, the headlights of the first of the vehicles began to appear.

Victoria bellowed and stamped her feet. Her cry brought help. Aunt Emily abandoned her vigil over

Cleopatra and the calf, and thudded her way out from the trees to join Victoria.

Side by side they began to walk towards the intruder.

Left to their own devices the rest of the herd huddled in a nervous cluster, peering anxiously out from the copse. The adults solicitously rumbled reassurance to their young and to each other, but the adolescents grunted fearfully nevertheless, picking up the message of apprehension.

As the vehicle approached them, the two elephants began to increase their speed. They raised their heads, flapped their ears back hard against their shoulders and broke into the prancing trot which precedes full charge.

But the charge never came. The confrontation faded as a second vehicle's lights began to emerge half a kilometre away to the left.

And a third to the right.

And a fourth.

The elephants slowed and shuffled to a halt, dismayed. They swung their heads from side to side, from one set of brightly burning eyes to another.

What to attack?

The danger was without focus, sliding towards them from too many sides.

And the confusion grew.

The steady pulse of the engines increased suddenly to violent roars, and the slow-moving vehicles began to pick up speed. Soon they were hurtling at the elephants from four directions, the lights bouncing and flashing, great clouds of dust being sucked up behind them as they came.

Intimidated and bemused, Emily began to back off.

Not yet quite defeated, Victoria stood her ground, making up her mind. Then, her instinct to protect her herd overcoming her fear, she took the only course available to her. Selecting the nearest of the rapidly approaching vehicles she raised her head angrily and proudly in the air, lifted her legs with astonishing lightness and grace into war-prance, and accelerated into full charge.

Within seconds she was thundering away from Emily.

And, as the space between elephant and vehicle rapidly lessened, Queen Victoria, more than six decades old, wise herd-mother, solicitous protector of generations of her kind, trumpeted a great bellow of challenge.

It was the last sound she was ever to make.

At that precise moment Laurens van der Wel squeezed the trigger of his automatic and, within a split second, six heavy bullets had splintered the side of Victoria's skull and smashed mercilessly into her brain.

In the casual, emotionless pressing of a small metal lever, nearly seventy years of life were brought to an end.

Victoria fell instantly.

Her head destroyed, she crashed to the ground with a massive, earth-shaking thud.

Probably she was dead before she fell, though her legs continued to run, in futile defiance of death, long after the vehicles, and the hard-faced, indifferent men they contained, had swept past her.

Probably, from the moment the bullets hit her, she would have seen and heard nothing.

Which was just as well for, had she been able to hear, she would not have been able to bear the anguished cries of the now leaderless, terrified herd as the vehicles roared around them in noisy circles, rounded them up into a crying, frantic babble of flesh, and began to move them away.

She would have had her great heart broken by the hoarse screams of a mortally afraid calf as he struggled, tiny and bewildered in his first hours of life, to keep pace with his profoundly frightened mother.

Victoria heard nothing.

But Papa Tembo did.

Though far, far away, he heard the shots. He heard the cries.

He turned his great head in terrible rage towards the sounds.

And before the herd was corralled within the horns of Cattle Rock, before the Bedford truck had been manoeuvred into position to block off the entrance to the enclosure, he was already on the move.

Which was, of course, exactly what Laurens van der Wel wanted.

He positioned his men high around the rocky walls of the enclosure, looking down upon the herd.

'Shoot any elephant that tries to escape,' he said.

Then, slowly, dragging his crippled leg, he climbed to the top of the point of one of the horns of rock.

He sat down, rested his gun across his knees and stared out across the plain.

'So,' he whispered to the heat-hazed, shimmering distances. 'I'm here.'

He narrowed his eyes against the glare of the high sun dancing on the shifting dust clouds.

Where are you?

TWENTY

'I had seen a herd of elephants . . . pacing along as if they had an appointment at the end of the world.'

Isak Dinesen, *Out of Africa*, 1937

'Hyram, I can't let you do this.'

Hyram was stamping, incandescent with anger, across the compound. He glared uncomprehendingly at Mike.

'Can't let me do it? It's my goddamn petrol, I'll do what I like with it. Get out of my way.'

'It's a criminal act.'

'So, big deal. I'm already a criminal, remember? Breaking and entering. And you know what? I don't care.'

'You might not care, Hyram. And if they throw you in jail again when you get back to New York, then fine, it'll keep you out of my hair for a while. But I'll tell you this – I've seen the inside of Tanzanian jails and my recommendation is that you give them a miss.'

'Thanks for your concern. I'm very touched. Now get out of the goddamn way.'

'It's not concern, it's self-protection. You want to spend five years in some stinking pit with rats and cockroaches crawling all over your head then that's your choice. But they might just decide to put Benny and me in there with you. So put that petrol can down.'

'Look behind you, Taylor, and tell me that what I'm doing isn't right. There's hundreds of tusks in that shed.'

'I know, Hyram, I know.'

'And that's just what's here *now*. Who knows how long he's been doing this? How many thousands have gone through here before? And all these other sheds. Look at them, man, look around you. Every goddamn thing that moves gets shot and ends up on a goddamn shelf in a goddamn hut. I knew he was a loony all along. I just didn't know how big a loony. He's a butcher. A psycho.'

'You know that and I know that. And I'm as sickened by him as you are. But if you just calm down and think for a minute, think *ahead* for a change, you might just possibly realize that burning all this to the ground destroys all the evidence. So when we get back to Arusha, what do we do? Tell the anti-poaching squad that van der Wel has been breaking the law and should be arrested, but unfortunately, because of a small fire, we can't prove it? I'll leave you to argue that one out with them.'

Hyram's eyes narrowed.

'I wasn't thinking of having him arrested,' he snarled. 'I was thinking of another, more permanent, cure.'

'First arson. Now murder. Very nice, Hyram. Just stop and take a look at yourself, will you. Take a long look at yourself and tell me what you see.'

The two men glared at each other for long moments. Finally Hyram dropped the petrol can, turned and walked away. He crossed the compound, slumped wearily down onto the ground, rested his back against the wall of one of the huts and put his head in his hands.

There was a long, long silence.

Benny unobtrusively collected the jerrycan and returned it to the Land Rover.

Eventually Hyram raised his head again. 'Do you remember,' he said quietly, 'those years ago, when we were chasing those other poachers, that I gave you a lecture about allowing anger to affect your judgement? I thought you were going to hit me that day.'

'I remember.'

'So, there we are then.'

'Yes,' said Mike gently, sitting down beside Hyram. 'There we are then.'

'Want to sock me on the jaw now? Teach me a lesson?'

'I want to sock you on the jaw most of the time, Hyram, but I never will because I'm a very mild-mannered, well-balanced, non-violent person.'

'And a schmuck into the bargain.'

They both smiled.

'You're right, of course,' Hyram continued. 'But look at it all. The thousands of things that have died. It's the pointlessness of it that gets me. The sheer, senseless, stupid destruction.'

'I know.'

'I'm not sentimental. You said the other night that I had to get things in proportion. That things were dying all the time out there. Everything's eating everything else, you said. But that's the way of things. That's Nature.'

'Yes.'

'This isn't right. This isn't natural. That goddamn shed's full of tusks. What's going on? There's more there than he could sell. The loony must be goddamn hoarding them. What are we going to do about him?'

'Now we've found him, we'll stop him. But we'll do it the right way and in a way that has the most effect.'

'What do you mean?'

'If we burn all this, it's gone for ever. If you shoot van der Wel as well then that's the end of the episode. Only you and I and Benny know anything about it. That's no good. People need to see what goes on. We're not just dealing with one man here. We're dealing with a hundred van der Wels right through Africa. We're dealing with a whole chain that ends in that shop you burgled in Manhattan, and shops like it all around the world. The chain finishes with the people with the fat wallets who buy the ivory. They're the ones who have to be stopped first.'

'So, how do we do that?'

'We catch van der Wel and let the law deal with him. The government will be delighted to make an example of him. It will show the world that they mean business about poaching and may well frighten others into retirement. And we take some photographs. You've got a camera that cost more than my Land Rover. Put it to some use. Get a record of all this and take it back to the States with you. Show the evidence to anyone who'll look. Show the newspapers. And, if you can overcome your natural shyness and reticence, you could use your mouth a bit too. Embarrass a few people. Ask the government what its policy is on ivory and skins, that sort of thing. Let people know. Educate them.'

'Yeah, I can see the sense in that,' Hyram replied. He sighed heavily. 'But that's all in the future. How long is it going to take for the message to seep through? I want to do something now.'

'I'm telling you what to do now. Get your camera and take some pictures.'

'Yeah, yeah, all right.'

Hyram heaved himself up onto his feet and started to walk back up the slope to the Land Rover. He was just passing through the compound gate when a sound brought him to a halt.

A faint, barely perceptible, rhythmic, metallic clacking from far away out on the plains.

It was over in a split second. But they all heard it and they all knew what it was.

The three men stood silently for a moment, looking out towards the sound, but it was not repeated.

Eventually Hyram nodded to himself.

'AK–47,' he said, quietly. 'If you didn't know.'

'Yep.' Mike agreed. 'AK–47.'

'I think perhaps I'll do this little photography job later,' Hyram announced.

He continued through the gate, stamped determinedly up to the Land Rover and climbed in.

'Anyone else coming?' he called, casually.

*

'Stop worrying about him, Alison.'

'I'm not worrying about him.'

'Yes you are. Don't lie. You haven't said a single word in the last two hours.'

Matt smiled at his sister. He was negotiating the Land Rover down a steep-sided water channel.

'We could be falling off the edge of a cliff here and you wouldn't have reacted. You're miles away.'

'Yes,' said John Blake from the back seat. 'You're unnaturally quiet. Bad sign.'

'All right, I am thinking about him. But I'm not worrying. I know they'll be looking after him. And before anybody says it, I know there's nothing we could do if they weren't. It's just that I want to be there, seeing what happens, seeing how he copes.'

'You will. We'll just stay one night at the Institute, load up with new food and water in the morning and we'll be back with the herd by late afternoon tomorrow. They'll still be where we left them. They all know that Cleopatra needs time to recover and that the calf can't travel far. They'll stay together. You'll see. Everything will be exactly as we left it.'

'I'd feel better if I'd seen him suckle. I hope he knows how to do it,' Alison remarked.

'He'll find out,' her father replied. 'They nearly all do. Cleopatra's healthy and there's been plenty of food, so she should have ample milk. And that sounds very much like worrying to me. If you're going to start worrying about him feeding then you've an awful long stretch in front of you. It'll be six months before he learns to feed from vegetation, and he could still be suckling in five years.'

'Oh.'

'Yes, "oh". Now take the advice I gave you. What will be, will be. We're observers. We watch and record. That's all.'

'Yes, Dad.'

They fell quiet again.

The Land Rover engine purred quietly, soporifically, as Matt eased it gently across the undulating ground.

John Blake closed his eyes and began to doze. Matt hummed softly to himself. Alison gazed through the windscreen, lost in her own thoughts.

And then, suddenly, without warning, it happened again, just as before.

Alison went icy cold and shivered.

'Oh!' she gasped.

Her hands went up to her mouth.

'Stop!' she said. 'Matt, stop the car!'

Matt reacted immediately to the alarm in her voice. He stamped on the brake and the Land Rover slid to a halt on the smooth grass.

'What's the matter? What is it?' he asked, looking around, thinking he had been about to run over something he hadn't noticed.

'What's going on?' mumbled John Blake sleepily. 'You nearly threw me off the seat.'

'Wait,' said Alison. 'Something's happened.'

'What are you talking about? What is it, for goodness' sake?'

'Matt, just shut up. *Please*.'

The urgency of her tone silenced Matt. He looked at her now with concern. John Blake pulled himself up straight on the back seat and watched her too.

She was frowning and staring hard out of the side window with complete concentration.

She remained silent for a long time.

Finally she whispered, barely audibly. Barely believing what was happening to her.

'He's there,' she whispered.

'Who?'

'The bull. He's there. And there's something wrong.'

So certain, so strange was her tone, that Matt felt the hair begin to rise on the back of his neck. He peered intently in the direction his sister was looking, but saw nothing.

Without speaking they opened the doors of the Land Rover and climbed out.

Alison walked away from the vehicle and stood gazing into the distance.

Her brother and father watched her as she silently searched the plain.

'There.'

She pointed.

They narrowed their eyes, staring hard at the horizon.

And eventually, far, far in the distance, they saw him. Small, but nevertheless unmistakable, heading east, back in the direction from which they had come, was the great bull.

He was moving steadily, conserving his strength, head down as though pushing through the air. Without hurry, but with machine-like determination.

Matt found that he was holding his breath. He exhaled, wonderingly.

'How? How on earth did you . . . ?'

'I don't know, Matt.' Alison almost snapped the reply. 'It's no good asking me. I don't understand any more than you do. I just knew, that's all.'

She stared hard at the bull, watching him carefully, reading his movements.

She shivered.

'An appointment at the end of the world,' she whispered.

'What?'

'He's heading back to the herd. There's something wrong.'

She turned to her father.

'He knows something's wrong. We have to go back. We have to go with him.'

John Blake looked into his daughter's eyes. The alarm, the concern in them, was tangible.

He nodded gently.

He did not understand what was happening and, for once, the scientist in him made no effort to understand.

Somehow Alison saw something he could not see, knew something that he could not know.

'Of course,' he said quietly, taking her hand and leading her back to the Land Rover. 'Of course we will.'

TWENTY-ONE

*'I cannot omit their care, to bury and cover the
carcasses of their companions, or any others
of their kind; for finding them dead they pass not
by them till they have lamented their common
misery, by casting dust and earth upon them . . .'*

Edward Topsell, *The History of Four-Footed Beasts*, 1607

Matt swung the Land Rover slowly round and headed
it across country at an angle. He approached to within
about half a kilometre of the bull, then he turned
again and allowed the vehicle to murmur gently along,
running parallel to the elephant, keeping pace with
him, but far enough away not to distract him.

The bull paid them little attention anyway. A brief
glance of appraisal and a perfunctory toss of the head
were the only signs that he had seen them at all. That
done, he ignored them.

So irrelevant were they to what was driving him
on that his pace did not slow at all.

They found that he was moving with surprising

rapidity. His great bulk moved with so little apparent effort. He *swept* over the ground, his feet barely lifting off the grass, but his legs surging forward in a long, distance-devouring rhythm.

The kilometres diminished rapidly.

The Land Rover, less agile than the elephant, less able to negotiate the gullies and outcrops of the difficult terrain, began to fall behind. The figure of the bull became smaller.

'It doesn't matter,' Matt said. 'There's no doubt where he's going. We'll soon find the herd. We'll catch him up there.'

'I'm frightened of what we'll find when we do.' Alison stared anxiously ahead through the windscreen. 'He's frightened too, I think. I wonder what it is he knows?'

John Blake patted his daughter's shoulder reassuringly, but said nothing. He knew it was a futile gesture. There was no reassurance to give.

'He's stopped,' said Matt. 'I'll see if I can close the gap a bit.'

He accelerated. The Land Rover bounced and thumped across open ground, its springs groaning in protest. When the elephant was once again clearly in their sights, he stopped.

'Can you see what he's doing?' John Blake asked.

'He's turning his head from side to side. He seems to have lost direction. As though he doesn't know which way to go.'

'Switch the engine off,' Alison said. 'Perhaps he can hear something.'

Matt turned the key and the engine died. They climbed out of the vehicle and stood, listening carefully. There was no sound but the metallic clicking of the engine, tortured by heat.

'Nothing,' said Matt eventually.

They stood in the silence, watching the bull. He remained stationary for long minutes. Only his head moved, now staring straight ahead, now swinging around to the left.

Then he made his decision. Abruptly, he pivoted to the left and set off at a trot. There was a new urgency in his movement.

Matt eased the Land Rover into gear and pulled the machine round in the direction the bull was taking.

Only then did they see what had caught the elephant's attention.

Alison's heart missed a beat.

'Oh no,' she murmured.

Far ahead, rotating slowly, with machine-like patience, a wheel of vultures ground a black circle on the powder-blue sky.

For a moment the occupants of the Land Rover went quiet, silenced as always by this macabre symbol, this daily reminder of the fragility of life and the horror of death.

'Don't jump to conclusions, Alison. It could be anything.'

'Don't be silly, Matt,' Alison replied.

She said it gently, without rancour, knowing her brother was only hoping, like her, that it would not be what they thought.

'If it was "anything" he wouldn't be heading for it.'

Matt braked. The Land Rover came to a halt.

'What are you doing?'

'Are you sure you want to go on?' Matt asked.

'Of course.'

'Sometimes it's better not to know.'

'No, it's not. It's never better not to know. Nothing is worse than imagination. If the calf's dead, then I want to know. I'll be able to handle it. I won't be able to handle wondering what happened to him and whether we could have saved him.'

'OK,' said Matt. 'So long as you're sure.'

'I'm sure. Let's go.'

The bull ran in a straight line for almost five kilometres and then slowed to a walk. In the last few hundred metres he became cautious, inspecting trees and hillocks and depressions in the ground before moving on.

The lifeless grey body pinned to the plain by the vultures' malign eyes had already attracted other opportunists. A pack of hyenas swirled excitedly around, chattering with anticipation, but without the courage to approach, waiting to see if lion or cheetah would want the first turn. Beyond the hyenas, marabou storks paced up and down on grotesque, skeleton legs, their bodies hunched like undertakers, their hands behind their backs.

Everything was assembling to take its place in the chain, everything joining the meal queue.

The bull snorted a peremptory warning as he approached the corpse. Then he stopped and waited for everything to obey him. The hyenas gave token resistance, chattering half-heartedly at him, but leaving the area immediately in a ragged, skittering flurry. They reassembled about half a kilometre away, grumbling insolently, periodically lifting their heads in unison in a strange ballet as they watched the elephant. The marabous' huge wings slapped the air lazily and the birds rose into nearby trees with the mournful *wap-wap* of wet cloth flapping.

Matt pulled the Land Rover up well away from the bull and switched the engine off.

Nobody spoke for a long time. For an age, it seemed, nobody knew what to say. It seemed incomprehensible that, in the short time since they had left the herd, something so cataclysmic could have occurred.

'Who is it?' Alison whispered finally.

'I don't know,' her father said quietly. 'I can't see clearly enough. It's one of the old ones. I don't know which.'

'I'll go and find out.'

Alison opened the door of the Land Rover. The bull turned his head and grunted at the sound of the door catch clicking.

'Stay where you are,' her father ordered. 'Who knows what's going on in his mind at the moment.'

'He won't harm me. And before either of you says anything – I know, that's all.'

Neither had time to reply before she had stepped out of the vehicle.

'I'm not going near. I'll leave them alone. I just want to see who it is.'

Matt and John Blake climbed out too. They stood by the Land Rover watching. Alison walked a few metres away from them and then stopped.

'What do you think?' Matt asked. 'Has it been a natural death or what?'

'I don't know,' his father replied. 'I can't tell from here. Though I suspect not.'

'Why?'

'The rest of the herd would still be here if it had been natural. There's no sign of them. That's ominous.'

He looked around nervously.

The bull had approached the dead elephant now and was standing motionless, towering above her corpse. He began to rumble gently and continuously, a soft vibration of sound, so deep it was felt rather than heard. He reached out his trunk and began to explore the still body.

Alison turned and whispered to her father and brother. 'I still can't see who it is.' Her voice trembled. 'I'm just going a little further.'

She walked on. The bull ignored her and continued exploring the lifeless body.

'Be careful,' said John Blake uselessly as he watched his daughter's slight figure receding.

He glanced at Matt, feeling foolish for having said it, but Matt merely raised his eyebrows and shrugged. To both of them it seemed wrong to let her go by herself – to watch her walk into potential danger without their protection. But what protection could be given?

Both men had come to the realization that they were excluded from what was happening. Whatever strange forces were at work between Alison and this great mysterious animal, they were not for them to know or understand.

They saw Alison stop about five metres from the elephants. They saw her hands come up to her head, the shoulders hunch and begin to heave with the sobs which rose through her body. They heard her sorrow and shock pulse back to them on the quiet air.

And they could do nothing for her, except wait and hurt with her.

She turned and walked back towards them, white faced.

John Blake stepped forward as she approached and enfolded her in his arms. She grasped him tightly.

'It's Victoria!' she whispered. 'Oh, Dad, she's got this terrible hole in her head. Someone's shot her. How could they? How could anyone do that?'

There was nothing her father could say to answer her question or to ease her pain. Just hold her tight and feel rage at the thought of how long his daughter, who had harmed nothing in her life, would have to carry the memory of this terrible sight.

Matt climbed up onto the bonnet of the Land Rover. From there he could see the scarlet blood which had flowed into a pool around Queen Victoria's head.

He clenched his hands, trying to hide his sorrow and rage and think clearly.

Because the big question was not, 'How could anyone do this?' The question was, 'Who did it?'

And where were they? Were they close by, watching them?

Where was the rest of the herd? Were they at this very moment in somebody's gun sights, on the point of being slaughtered?

He climbed higher, up onto the roof, and looked around.

Nothing. The plains were empty for as far as he could see in every direction.

He was just about to climb down and suggest they went looking for the rest of the herd when an extraordinary thing happened. The bull gave a soft bellow and began to paw the ground at Victoria's side.

They all watched as he thudded his great foot into the earth and drew it back. Again and again his foot crashed down and scraped at the earth. He was excavating a furrow beside Victoria's lifeless body. Gradually, as he drove deeper, he entered the water-table. The soil became moist at first, then, as he continued, wet. Water started to seep into the hole he was digging and soon they could hear the slurping and sucking of mud.

'What's he doing?' Matt asked, wonderingly.

As if in answer, the bull, who had now excavated a hole about a metre deep and the same in length, reached down with his trunk, scooped up a quantity of mud and, with infinite gentleness, laid it in the terrible gaping hole in Queen's Victoria's head. He carefully smoothed out the mud with his trunk, pressing it into the wound, then turned, reached down into the hole for more and repeated the action.

Alison gasped.

'Look!' she said. 'Look what he's doing. He's treating her wound. Oh, the poor thing. He doesn't understand. He doesn't know she's dead. He's trying to help her.'

'No,' said John Blake, gently. 'He knows.'

'What's he doing then?'

'He's in shock.'

'Shock?'

'Yes. I've seen it before. It's exactly the same thing that humans do when they lose someone they love. In their mind they know the person's gone, but at first the heart won't accept it. They think a miracle will happen and the person will come back to life again if they're just given a little encouragement. When people die, the living often continue talking to them for ages. Telling them that things will be all right, telling them not to worry, telling them to come back. That sort of thing. Denial. It's a natural part of the grieving process. Humans do it and elephants do it too.'

Matt narrowed his eyes and stared at his father in astonishment.

' "If you think you can drag me into a discussion about animals' feelings . . ." ' he muttered under his breath.

'So let's leave him to his grief, shall we?' John Blake went on. 'We need to decide what to do next. It needs careful thinking out. We could be in danger ourselves.'

He put his arm around Alison's shoulders and began to lead her back to the Land Rover.

The bull briefly stopped what he was doing. He rumbled gently, then swung his great head round and watched them move away.

Alison felt his soft eyes come to rest upon her.

She stopped and turned to look at him.

They remained motionless for a long time, locked in a strange, silent communion.

Finally Alison nodded, as though to herself.

'It's not over,' she said. 'This is not what he came for . . . not the appointment he had to keep.'

She looked up into her father's eyes.

'The decisions are already made for us. He knows what to do. This is only the beginning.'

TWENTY-TWO

*'What happens to beasts will happen to Man.
All things are connected. If the great beasts are
gone, man would surely die of a great loneliness
of spirit.'*

Chief Seattle of the Nez Percé, 1884

Late afternoon.

Benny halted the Land Rover and the three men climbed out. From the top of the low escarpment they could look out towards the horizon.

They shuffled around dispiritedly, knowing the day was nearing its close. The tracks they had followed had vanished over an hour ago. So they had driven blind. Kept the Land Rover pointing east and hoped.

An argument had developed over where the shots had come from. There had been a lot of shouting.

Eventually the moment had come when they had had to admit, sourly, that they had lost their quarry.

Hyram sighed wearily and slumped down onto the ground, disappointed. The heaviness of the afternoon hours had dulled the sharp edge of his anger and replaced it with torpor.

Now, as he looked out across the silent plains, washed lion-coloured by the amber sun, even he, ever optimistic, ever irascibly determined, began to feel cowed, defeated by the scale of Africa.

'So, what's the goddamn point?' he muttered to himself.

'What?'

A long pause as Hyram continued staring at something invisible at great distance.

'Just thinking aloud,' he said eventually. 'Just wondering what I'm doing careering around like this at the end of the world. Wondering who *is* the loony, him or me.'

'Now there's a question that's been exercising my mind for some time,' mused Mike.

'And wondering what difference I think I can make. Wondering if it isn't just a bit goddamn *arrogant* that I'm here at all.'

'Well, well. Things have taken a turn. Is this *humility* I'm listening to? Is this Hyram T. Johnson *doubting* himself? I find that very difficult to cope with.'

'Look out there, Taylor. Tell me what you see.'

'Nothing much out of the ordinary.' Mike shrugged.

'I know. That's the point. It's just as it's been for millions of years. The only difference now is that *we're* here. You've seen there's a rhino down there?'

'Yep. She knows we're here. She's pushed her calf around the back of the tree.'

'Suppose a gang of *shifta* turned up now and tried

to shoot the goddamn thing and get her horn. What would we do?'

'Er . . . I'd politely request them not to do any such thing.'

'Yeah, 'course you would. And I'd stand behind you and say "please" too. And they'd go away and we'd have saved it and we'd be proud. And we'd slap ourselves on the backs and move on. Then what?'

'What do you mean, "then what"?'

'What about tomorrow? When the men come back. Because men like that always do come back. That poor half-blind thing down there, trying to protect its calf, has been harried virtually out of existence. Just for its horn. If people are that goddamn stupid then there's no hope. So in the long run what does it matter if we're here or not? Won't things just take their course, in spite of anything we do? Everything's going to die anyway. So, what's the point?'

'You've got a touch of what they call the "Africa wins again" syndrome. It happens to us all at some stage. The country gets to you. You start to feel that it's in charge. That it controls your life. It floods just to spite you personally, so you can't get where you want to go. It picks out your tyres as the ones it will puncture. It makes planes break down just as you're getting on them. That sort of thing. Come on, Hyram, you're depressed because we've lost the trail. That's par for the course for us anyway. You've always grumbled about my tracking abilities.'

'What tracking abilities?' Hyram muttered.

'Exactly. Now listen. I can barely put up with the normal foul-tempered, coarse, pig-headed, egotistical, demanding, loud-mouthed Hyram Johnson. A Hyram

Johnson weeping into his handkerchief is more than anyone can stand.'

'Taylor, you should come down off the fence. Let me know what you really think of me sometime,' said Hyram mildly.

He went quiet again.

'Have you got children?' Mike asked eventually.

'Two. Son and daughter. Grown up now, of course. And four grandchildren.'

'Perhaps that's what you're doing here then. Imagine a world where your grandchildren couldn't see an elephant or a rhino, except as a picture in a book. And at the foot of the page the word "extinct". Isn't that what you're doing here? What we're all doing here?'

Hyram nodded.

'Yeah, I guess. It's just that what we can do seems so small, so insignificant.'

'It's a start, Hyram. And others follow. Cheer up. We'll find van der Wel tomorrow. By the time we've finished with him you'll feel what we've done is significant, I promise you that.'

'OK, I'll take your word for it. So, I suppose we might as well go on a bit. We'll try and find somewhere decent to camp for the night.'

He hauled himself laboriously to his feet. He took a last look at the motionless rhino. Her calf had emerged and joined her. They stood together, close, staring out challengingly with fierce, heroic blindness, their grey shadows almost imperceptible, absorbed into the bark of the tree.

Hyram shook his head sadly. Then he looked up at the sky.

'And there's another thing that's depressing me,' he said.

'What?'

'Vultures. I'm sick of goddamn vultures. Everywhere you go in Africa there's goddamn vultures.'

He regarded the distant wheel of birds malevolently for a moment. Then, abruptly, he spat on the ground and started walking back to the Land Rover.

'Come on,' he said. 'Let's go and take a look at what they've found. With a bit of luck it's van der Wel, shot himself. Now that would cheer me up.'

Laurens van der Wel became increasingly impatient as the afternoon wore on.

His men recognized the signs of trouble brewing. First the hardening of the face into a set, expressionless mask. Then the narrowing of the eyes. Finally, the restless, tormented pacing.

From their stations, ranged on the rocky hillside around the edges of the enclosure, the men watched him limping backwards and forwards. Silhouetted against the sky, isolated by his lonely obsession, his strange, twisting gait was the essence of childhood nightmare. The lurching, poisonous troll of fairy tale, whose heavy feet shuffle, with claustrophobic resonance, in all our dreams.

Sher-*thunk*. Sher-*thunk*. Sher-*thunk*.

The men averted their eyes and closed their ears to him.

The elephants had eventually gone quiet. They moved hesitantly and fearfully about their prison, their anxiety manifesting itself in different ways.

Some huddled together, silent and disconsolate, seeking comfort in company.

Some called softly to each other with 'Where are you?', 'Here I am' rumbles, trying to reassure, to convince that things would turn out for the best.

Some of the males on the thresholds of maturity periodically glanced upward at the men ringing them, and wondered, and assessed. But in the end their emerging bull's instinct for battle was not yet strong enough to overcome their adolescent fear.

Cleopatra tended, as best she could, to her calf, which lay trembling at her feet, slowly recovering from his ordeal. Every so often she would touch him with her trunk to still his fear.

Aunt Emily stood nearby but, fearful and profoundly shocked herself, she had nothing to offer except her presence.

Some attempted to restore normality to the day by behaving as if nothing had happened. They wandered about the enclosure grazing, apparently calm and unconcerned. But they fooled no one, not even themselves.

Lost without Queen Victoria's guidance, the herd knew that there was nothing to be done but wait.

Alison Blake sat with her back against a tree, watching Papa Tembo, waiting with him.

He had buried Queen Victoria.

When he had finished packing her wound, he had kicked earth over her body, gradually covering her. Then he had ripped branches from the nearby trees and gently laid them over her.

That completed he simply stood by her, for all

the world as though he kept a lonely vigil, his soft rumblings breathing a quiet requiem on the heavy afternoon air.

Alison stared at the massive figure engaged in his solitary, sorrowful task and shook her head with wonder.

'It's exactly the same,' she said. 'He can't dig a hole like we do, but apart from that it's the same. We bury people in the earth and put flowers on their graves. That's just what he's done.'

'It's the strangest thing about them,' John Blake whispered. 'They understand death. There's no doubt about that. I've seen this dozens of times. They'll pass by the remains of any other animal without a glance. But if they come upon another dead elephant, the whole herd will react. Even dry, bleached bones that have been there for months, they'll stop and examine them. I've seen them pick up bones and skulls and pass them around. I'd swear they were trying to identify who it had been.'

'There's something on his mind as well. He keeps lifting his head, have you noticed?' Matt asked.

'Hmm. He's listening, I think. He knows where the others are. He changed direction to get here to Victoria, remember. I think he's just keeping an ear open on them. He doesn't seem in a hurry now.'

'He's waiting,' said Alison. 'I'm not sure what for. Darkness perhaps. We must wait with him. When he goes, we'll go.

Laurens van der Wel's patience finally snapped.

He called one of his men over.

'Torch the grass,' he said, looking down upon the herd in the enclosure.

There was no expression in his voice, or in his eyes. He delivered the instruction simply, without emotion.

'Burn them alive.'

He turned and looked out across the plain again.

'Enough waiting,' he murmured to the lowering, heat-heavy distance. 'Flush him out.'

TWENTY-THREE

'We are the fire which burns the country.
The calf of the elephant is exposed on the plain.'

Bantu saying

Aunt Emily's nostrils quivered as she picked up the first faint waftings of the smoke.

Cleopatra turned her head, sensing Emily's unease.

Emily snorted, not yet fully recognizing the threat. The rest of the herd stopped what they were doing and turned questioningly, trying to ascertain what had disturbed her. The adolescent males started to stamp restlessly, wondering what was happening.

Cleopatra pulled her calf closer to her side and stroked him with her trunk, murmuring gently to calm his instinctive fear.

Then Emily recognized the threat for what it was and delivered the warning – the half-challenge, half-terror bellow of extreme danger.

Run! Get away!

The news spread quickly.

Within minutes of the first innocent-looking blue

strands of smoke beginning to twist upwards into the air, every creature within a radius of ten kilometres knew about it.

The elephants instantly passed the message among themselves with shocked urgency. Their rumblings floated out over the walls of their prison. Vibrations of warning pulsed out on the air and, like radio waves, were picked up by a million sensitively tuned receivers.

Heads turned enquiringly.

Voices called and were answered.

Mouths ceased their endless chewing of food and were still.

Hoofs began to dance, at first uncertain which way to go, but knowing the vibrations said 'run'.

And then the message clarified as the smoke began to stain the sky.

Calls became bellows and roars of command, summoning the absent, gathering the wanderers. The first low grumblings of a rolling thunder began to echo, hollowly, in the ground as countless animals drew together, like with like, and started to move away from the danger. A thunder which would grow and shake the earth as they accelerated away and flowed, like water, across the plain.

Lakes of wildebeest; rivers of gazelle and shimmering zebra; the lolloping giraffe and tumbling baboon; the ponderous, meat-heavy lion; the swift cheetah and skittering hyena; all moving together, in liquid unison and with single purpose.

Escape.

'What's going on?' asked Hyram, looking out of the side window of the Land Rover and watching the line of wildebeest bucking and prancing in panicked flight along the skyline. 'Where are all those animals going in such a hurry?'

'I don't know,' Mike answered. 'It's not "where" that interests me anyway, it's "why".'

Benny braked and pulled the Land Rover up.

'See, *bwana*,' he said. 'Look ahead. Smoke in the sky.'

'There,' said Mike, smiling. 'Happy now, Hyram? That's their cooking fire, I guess. Got out of hand a bit perhaps. I knew van der Wel would give himself away eventually.'

Hyram nodded.

'So, let's go visiting,' he said.

Benny swung the Land Rover round and headed towards the smoke.

'What's happening?' asked Matt Blake, leaning forward away from the trunk of the tree he had been resting against. 'I can feel a vibration. Coming up through the ground into the tree.'

'I don't know,' John Blake answered, listening carefully. 'Sounds like something's being stampeded. Lion attacking something, I guess.'

He moved out, away from the tree and scanned the plain.

'What the . . . ?' he said.

Animals were on the move everywhere.

His eyes searched in the direction from which they were fleeing.

Dark smoke was just beginning to rise into view.

'Matt!' he said. 'Come and look.'

*

'What is it?' Alison enquired, in a whisper, of Papa Tembo.

She was seated, cross-legged on the ground, a few feet away from him.

The atmosphere of the afternoon had changed with startling abruptness. Abandoning his vigil, the bull had suddenly lifted his head and extended his trunk high into the air.

She watched him carefully.

His body had tensed, his muscles suddenly taut.

Alison got to her feet.

'Is it time now?' she asked him. 'Is it time to go?'

The bull snorted once, turned and padded away through the trees.

In seconds he was gone, silently, as though dissolved into air.

Alison ran back to the Land Rover.

'Quickly!' she ordered. 'He's moving.'

Laurens van der Wel watched, face impassive, as his men set the fires and they began to take hold.

Thick smoke began to appear in different parts of the enclosure. The elephants moved uncertainly this way and that, hearing the warnings the big, old cow had given, sniffing the smoke for themselves with raised, questioning trunks but unable at first to decide what to do.

But, as the smoke thickened, uncertainty quickly gelled into fear.

The younger elephants began to run instinctively, for terror of fire, the great obliterator, is embedded in race memory. They shouted out in panic, some running *towards* the fire, for fear has no direction, panic is blind.

A cold half-smile began to play around van der Wel's mouth. This was unexpectedly entertaining.

Two or three elephants detached themselves from the herd and started to run across to the other side of the enclosure, where they were met by sheer blank walls of dark rock. Others started to make their way further in, heading for where the rocks narrowed at the furthest end of the amphitheatre about half a kilometre away.

To where his men were already setting another fire.

Van der Wel's lip curled, bending the smile into a sneer. Long-forgotten childhood words crept into his head.

'Three blind mice,' he whispered, watching a group of elephants run into a fissure in the rocks, where they would surely trap themselves.

'Three blind mice,' he sniggered again, shaking his head at the cow who was futilely pushing and prodding a new-born calf with her tusks, trying to urge it to its feet.

'They all ran after the farmer's wife,' he snorted as he watched a big, old cow dashing confusedly this way and that, desperately, but completely ineffectually, trying to gather her herd together and protect them.

His eyes moved around the enclosure, scanning the progress of the fire. It was beginning to take hold on the east side. The grass was heavy and dense, and blue smoke was massing and consolidating in thick clouds. Brief talons of flame flashed through the smoke and he could hear the satisfying hiss and rumble and crackle which is the song of gathering fire.

He rose to his feet, beginning now to lose interest

in the joke he was playing on these stupid animals. They were dashing aimlessly in all directions.

He glanced down into the enclosure a final time. A group of young elephants was trying to scale a steep slab of rock. In desperation they would scramble a few metres upwards, then the incline would defeat them and they would slide and tumble miserably down again, screeching in despair.

But they kept trying. Mindlessly trying, time and time again.

'Did you ever see such a thing in your life?' van der Wel marvelled, his voice coldly contemptuous.

The prancings and antics were just too ridiculous. The clumsy cavortings of these great, ugly, grey clowns so brainless that they were hardly even funny.

Never mind. They were making a noise. That was what mattered.

He turned his back on them, leaving the doomed herd to its graceless, galumphing dance towards death.

No wonder they use them in circuses, he thought, as he climbed back up onto the hill's crest.

He walked to the edge of the slope and sat down on a rock, staring out over the plain. His eyes moved restlessly back and forth along the horizon.

Eventually, sensing rather than seeing something, he raised his binoculars to his eyes.

He smiled. 'Ah,' he breathed.

For, even at great distance, there was no mistaking him.

His immense size, the angry cast of his great head, the thrust of shoulders of incomprehensible power, the glint of the late, reddening sun on his massive tusks, left no room for doubt.

It was him.

The plan had worked. He was on his way.

'Come,' said Laurens van der Wel, softly. 'Come, my little blind mouse.'

He sat down, laid his gun across his knees and willed himself to wait calmly.

This time there must be no error of judgement, no possibility of failure.

His finger gently caressed the safety catch of the gun.

'Come, Papa Tembo,' he whispered again. 'And I'll cut off your tail with my carving knife.'

TWENTY-FOUR

'Epwo m-baa pokin in-gitin' got.'
Everything has an end.

Maasai saying

'Stop, Benny.'

The Land Rover came to a halt. Benny left the engine running.

The men sat, looking ahead. They were about a kilometre from the source of the smoke.

'Hell,' said Hyram, quietly.

It was an observation, not a profanity.

Fire creates its own turbulence, its own winds. The smoke ascending from Cattle Rock was gripped by its own heat, contorted into spirals and pushed down again. It billowed and somersaulted in twisted ropes down the steep hill-slopes and crept outwards onto the plain, rolling like fog across the ground. The dying sun, dissolving behind the hill, splashed stains of crimson onto the smoke so that what was visible of the hill was etched black between a shifting sea of red and a blood-washed sky.

Hell on earth.

'Some goddamn cooking fire that, Taylor. What do you think? Is it accidental or what?'

'I don't know. Let's see what we can see.'

Mike Taylor picked up the binoculars. He opened the Land Rover door, climbed out and walked a few paces away from the vehicle. He was adjusting the focus when Hyram joined him.

'Come on, come on,' said Hyram impatiently.

Mike panned the glasses slowly along the hill. Smoke obscured much of it, but here and there pinnacles of jagged rock jutted up like blackened, rotting teeth.

In the spectral, reddening light it was hard to know what was reality and what was illusion. Solid rock dissolved into smoke, smoke coalesced into figures, which melted quickly back into smoke again.

'What do you see?'

'I don't know. Nothing. Something. Impressions. I think there's somebody on the rim of the hill. That's a big fire though.'

'Do you think it's van der Wel?'

'Almost certainly. The Maasai wouldn't be grass-burning in there. But what he's up to I have no idea.'

At that moment Benny turned the key in the ignition and the softly throbbing engine became silent.

It took a second or two for their ears to adjust. But when they did, they heard the faint sounds that the engine had been masking.

The muted, low rumble of distant fire rolled over the plain towards them, counterpointing the high wails of the trapped animals; calls of anguish and terror that distance could not diminish.

The cries of tormented souls trapped in Hell.

'My God!' said Mike, barely believing what he heard. 'That's elephant. He's got elephant in there!'

Hyram drew in his breath sharply with shock.

'What ... is ... the goddamn loony ... doing?' he hissed.

The lid of the ammunition box rattled behind them, followed by the clicks of bullets being pressed into their clips.

'Yes, Benny, that's right,' said Mike quietly, without turning.

Hyram began to walk back to the vehicle.

'You going to give me another goddamn lecture about arson and murder, Taylor?' he asked.

'No, Hyram,' Mike answered.

Anger stretched his face tight and constricted his voice. He climbed into the driving seat and started the engine. Benny remained in the back, loading the guns.

The Land Rover lurched forward as Mike stamped his foot hard on the accelerator and released the clutch pedal with a vicious thump.

'Bwana?'

Van der Wel did not turn.

'What?'

'Bwana,' the Mchawi continued, 'we must go.'

There was a long pause before a reply came.

'Go?' Van der Wel was incredulous, uncomprehending.

The Mchawi watched him warily.

Van der Wel was strangely quiet.

'Yes, bwana. This, that we have done, it is bad. It is too much. People are coming. We have seen vehicles in the distance. They come to see what causes the smoke. We must go.'

'Vehicles?' Van der Wel shrugged dismissively. 'What vehicles? What people?'

He seemed distant, as though the words he heard meant nothing to him.

The Mchawi stepped forward, hoping he could persuade the man to move away, but van der Wel swung round and faced him with such sudden violence that he retreated again.

'If there are people,' van der Wel hissed, 'then we will dispose of them.'

He was icy calm and spoke so softly that he was barely audible.

The Mchawi stepped back again. His hands began to tremble and the back of his neck prickled with fear. The man was too calm, too controlled. It was unnatural.

'Yes, *bwana*,' he agreed.

He began to back slowly away.

'I will tell the men, *bwana*.'

He searched van der Wel's eyes, seeking a clue as to what this deeply unnerving man might do.

The eyes stared blankly back at him, giving nothing away, but by their very inexpression increasing the possibility of terrible violence. The calm was the still centre of the hurricane. The worst was yet to come.

The Mchawi turned on his heels and vanished into the smoke.

Van der Wel watched him go.

Briefly he glanced down through the smoke into the boiling cauldron below.

The cries of the elephants seemed quieter, less

fearful, as though they were slowly becoming resigned to their fate and facing their inevitable destruction with equanimity.

As the smoke swirled and shifted, the herd was now revealed, now concealed again. They were bunched together, driven gradually further and further towards the centre of the amphitheatre as the fire crept inexorably inwards.

Van der Wel watched for a moment or two, then his eyes began to sting and he started coughing. He returned to his lookout point on the edge of the hill. But now he could see nothing. The plain was shrouded by great shifting banks of smoke swirling away into the distance.

He sneered and laughed softly to himself. But this time the sneer was directed within, at his own thoughtless stupidity.

The joke had turned sour.

'Three blind mice,' he snarled, his voice heavy with sarcasm.

The smoke continued still, rolling implacably down the hillsides. Dense, stinging, impenetrably heavy, it obscured the ground, devoured the trees, shrouded the sky. It gripped the sun and squeezed the life from it.

Blinding smoke.

And in the smoke, somewhere, Papa Tembo.

Van der Wel could feel him there.

But now the tables were turned. Silent and weightless as a cloud, his great body smoke-coloured, the bull moved, insubstantial, invisible, across the plain, now here, now there, a swirling smoke-shadow, a shifting shade.

Approaching unseen, step by unheard step, nearer, nearer, nearer.

Laurens van der Wel snarled with rage that his own hand, his order, had given the bull this sanctuary.

'Damn you!' he shouted into the smoke. 'Damn you!'

The snarl became a scream of anguish that once again he could fail, that once again Papa Tembo could outwit him.

Again and again he screamed at the darkening plain.

'Damn you! Damn you! Damn you! Damn you!'

His men watched him for a while then, shaking their heads at the spectacle of this strange figure raging at nothing, quietly turned their backs and crept away.

So no one saw van der Wel tie a scarf around his face as protection from the acrid smoke and descend the hillside into the swirling grey sea.

No one heard his feet crunching on the rocky scree or the clink of the gun as he steadied himself against the rocks.

No one heard him muttering to himself as he walked to the entrance of the amphitheatre and took up position by the truck which blocked the opening.

No one, that is, except Papa Tembo, whose sensitive ears could hear the man breathing at a mile, whose trunk could have sniffed him out and positioned him with pinpoint accuracy at two, and whose other sense, the one we call the sixth, would have known he was there from a hundred.

Van der Wel peered into the smoke.

He shivered, momentarily dismayed.

'Who's the blind mouse now?' he whispered to himself.

'Where is he?' Matt asked.

He had stopped the Land Rover.

'I don't know. I lost sight of him between those trees,' John Blake replied.

Alison stared straight ahead. The bank of smoke was drifting slowly towards them.

'He's in the smoke now.' Her voice faltered, cracked with emotion. Her hands were up to her ears as she tried to shut out the terrible cries which floated from the distant hill. But it was futile. The cries chilled her, froze her flesh to her bones with horror at the thought of what was happening.

Her eyes tried to penetrate the greyness, tried to separate the bull from the shifting smoke.

'We must go after him. He'll need our help.'

John Blake shook his head.

'Alison, we can't.'

Shocked, Alison turned and looked up at her father.

'Can't? Why?'

John Blake put his arm gently around his daughter's shoulders.

'Think a moment. About the people who have done this thing. Why they have done it I have no idea. But in forty years in Africa I have never seen anything worse done to animals. Never. And they are still there. Invisible in the smoke.'

'We have guns,' Matt interrupted. 'We know how to use them.'

'Matt, please. Back me up. You know it's no good.

We don't know who they are or how many. There could be twenty of them for all we know. And they'll shoot first and ask who we were later. Or, more likely they'll shoot first and never bother to ask who we were. I won't risk our lives. I can't.'

'And so we stay alive,' countered Alison. 'And afterwards?'

'What do you mean?'

'For the next fifty years can we live with ourselves, knowing we walked away from this? Listen to their cries. That's the herd that's been your life. And mine and Matt's. Listen! That's Aunt Emily and Boxer and Hamlet. It's Cleopatra and her baby. Listen to them. They're dying. Listen!'

'I know. And part of us will die with them. But for God's sake, Alison, try and see things from my point of view too. What sort of father would knowingly put his children in danger?'

'We're not children. We can make up our own minds.' Alison's face had hardened with determination.

'You'll always be children to me. When you're forty you'll still be my children. And I'll still be worrying about you and trying to keep you safe.'

Alison stared hard at her father. Her eyes faded from anger to incomprehension to compassion.

'I understand,' she said, after a long pause. 'Of course, I understand.'

She turned and stared at the rolling bank of smoke. She spoke softly, almost as though to herself.

'So, I'm sorry. If things turn out badly, I'm sorry. But he needs my help. I don't know what I can do, but I know he needs me. I can't ignore that.'

And she set off running.

214

It was so sudden, so unexpected, that it took the two men completely by surprise. She was several metres away before they had even registered what was happening.

'Dear God!' Matt gasped.

'Oh no! Please, no!' John Blake started to run after her, his heart thudding against his ribs with shock.

'*Alison!*' he screamed.

He pounded after her.

But it was useless. Alison could run like the wind. She knew it and they knew it.

Within seconds she had disappeared into the swirling smoke.

Immediately John Blake abandoned the chase, turned and started running back to the Land Rover. Matt had already started the vehicle and was swinging it round to head towards the smoke. He barely slowed as John Blake pulled open the passenger door and hauled himself in. He floored the accelerator pedal and roared away.

'Find her, Matt! Please God, find her quickly.'

'The entrance is at the south-west end,' Benny said. 'It's very narrow. No more than about five metres across. If he wanted to block it he could do so easily.'

Mike was negotiating the Land Rover slowly through the smoke towards Cattle Rock.

'To what purpose?' he asked. 'That's what baffles me. What use is it if they burn to death? Where's the ivory then? Where's his profit in that?'

'I don't know,' replied Hyram. It was almost a snarl. 'What's more, I don't goddamn care. Since when did loonies need a reason for anything? What you going to do? Write a goddamn book about him? Just get there, will you? Never mind reasons.'

'I'm going as fast as I can, Hyram,' Mike snapped back. 'Look ahead, will you? You can see what visibility's like. If I smash the sump off on a rock we'll be going nowhere.'

The headlights cut yellow channels through the eerily swirling smoke. The sun, settling now into the horizon, painted the world dark red. The lights of gathering twilight were those of fire and smoke.

Shadowy trees, black and spectral, stepped forward and receded as they crept slowly along.

Perspectives altered, so that Mike would swerve for dark looming rocks, only to see them dissolve and swirl away, or drive through a patch of dark smoke lying on the grass to have the front wheels crash down into a hollow in the ground.

'Things aren't what they seem, Hyram.'

Suddenly, out of the smoke, headlights emerged, travelling at great speed. Mike braked sharply. The vehicle roared directly at them, swerved violently at the very last second, and thundered past, missing them by a hair's breadth.

'Jeez,' said Hyram. 'That, unless I'm mistaken, was exactly what it seemed.'

'All black men, I think,' observed Benny. 'No *mzungu* with them.'

'We're going to lose him!' Hyram snapped. 'They're all pulling out of here. Jeez, after all this, we're going to lose him.'

'They've seen us coming probably. Think we're the anti-poaching squad, perhaps. Anyway, the priority is the elephants. Though God knows what we can do.'

'Keep goddamn going, that's what you can do.'

Mike engaged gear and set off again. They had gone barely fifty metres more when there was a series of metallic thuds and the explosive tinkling of shattering glass.

And before they had time to register what was happening there was a single tremendous bang, the whole vehicle shuddered from end to end and lurched to a violent halt. The occupants were hurled forward.

'Whoa,' said Hyram as his forehead banged on the windscreen. He pushed himself back into his seat. 'What was that?'

A loud hissing sound almost drowned his voice. Clouds of steam poured out from the sides and front of the bonnet.

'Oh no!' said Mike. 'Stay there a minute. If that was what I think it was . . .'

Hyram ignored him and climbed out. He walked round to the front of the Land Rover and surveyed the damage. A horizontal line of holes stretched across the front of the vehicle. Unmistakably bullet holes. They had punched through the wings and shattered the headlights.

Hyram squatted down on his haunches and peered through the grille. The radiator was holed in three places. Pressurized water squirted in hissing jets from the holes, and steam poured out to mingle with the smoke. Hot oil dripped onto the grass from the cracked engine block.

Hyram heaved himself upright again, walked round to the driver's side and addressed Mike through the open window.

'Yup,' he said, matter-of-factly. 'It was what you thought it was.'

'Right,' said Mike. 'Let's get out of here.'

He opened the door and slid out. Benny climbed out of the back door and passed them each a gun.

'No rush,' said Hyram, peering nonchalantly into the smoke. 'They can't see us, any more than we can see them. They shot into the smoke at our headlights, that's all. They've killed the lights stone dead. Real smart guys. Now they've got no target no more.'

'Maybe,' snapped Mike. 'But they know where they just aimed. If they fire off another volley in the same direction they might just be lucky enough to hit one of us. Given our respective sizes it's more likely to be you, Hyram, than me or Benny. If you take my advice you'll get away from the Land Rover.'

He started to move away.

'I'll take my chance. Don't get so worked up, Taylor. You've seen too many Hollywood films. It's hard enough to hit a man when you're aiming at him. Just firing off at nothing it's a million-to-one chance you'll hit anything. So let's shut up a minute, listen, and gather our senses.'

Mike and Benny stopped. The three men stood silent, listening. The smoke swirled around them, irritating their throats, making their eyes water. Momentarily it parted to reveal trees and rocks, then closed in upon them again. Like fog it had a deadening effect on sound.

There was less noise from the elephants anyway now. The low susurrating roar, the tread of travelling fire, pervaded everything, but now it was punctuated only by intermittent, solitary calls.

But they were calls of such distress that they gripped the heart.

The cries of baffled, harried beasts in extremity; of tortured creatures aproaching the last precipice, looking at the final edge of life. *And knowing that they did so*.

But there was another sound too. The sound which came from behind them.

So soft it was barely heard.

'Bwana,' whispered Benny.

Mike felt the hair rise on the back of his neck.

'I hear it,' he replied.

Sluff. Sluff. Sluff. Sluff.

The sound of great feet sliding through grass.

Hyram's hands began to tremble. He turned slowly. Time seemed to stretch and bend. His turning seemed to take minutes.

He glanced sideways at Mike and Benny. They were silent and motionless. Transfixed.

Hyram stared hard into the obscuring smoke.

The last, smouldering embers of the setting sun stained the swirling smoke with slashes of dusk-red, so that the great primeval head, as it took shape and clarified, seemed to emerge from fire itself.

Hyram drew in his breath sharply.

He had lived this moment before.

The same head emerging, the same body taking shape, the whole immense, incomprehensibly powerful bulk *coalescing*, as though it were being created, being *made* here and now before his very eyes, out of the fire and smoke itself.

But this time there was no distance separating

them. This time there were no binoculars to diminish him, or to take his reality away.

This time the great bull was here, in heart-stopping proximity.

Hyram stepped back involuntarily and his stomach lurched with fear. The great beast had appeared so suddenly, so quietly.

Hyram's mouth fell open in awe.

The whispering lightness of the delicate feet gave lie to the immensity of the being that glided towards him. Three times the height of a man, six tonnes in weight – implacable, prehistoric, unstoppable, he seemed to Hyram to be, quite literally, elemental. To be built of rock and air and fire.

Profoundly, awesomely frightening.

The three men instinctively raised their guns as the bull approached.

'Get behind me,' Mike whispered to the other two. He settled the stock of the .416 firmly against his shoulder, raised the barrel and took aim.

Hyram remembered Mike's words.

'Big enough to knock the engine out of a car, this one.'

The words held no comfort.

'Try not to shoot, Taylor,' he said.

'I won't unless I have to. He might leave me no choice.'

And then, astonishingly, without giving them so much as a passing glance, the elephant was gone. He vanished, melted away as though he had never been, silent and weightless as the smoke itself.

There was a pause, until the men breathed again and the world resumed its normal pace.

'Jeez,' whispered Hyram, finally. He gripped the

stock of his gun firmly to still the trembling of his hands. 'That was a narrow escape. He didn't even notice us. He went straight by without seeing us.'

'No,' said Mike, shaking his head. 'He saw us. He didn't have time for us, that's all. We're irrelevant to him.'

'That's the one I saw. The one who killed the Maasai herdsman. That's him, Papa Tembo. The one they wanted you to shoot.'

'I know.'

They stared at the point where the animal had vanished. Imagination gave brief solidity to the swirling greyness. The elephant's great bulk formed, dissolved and re-formed in their minds' eyes.

'He's come to help, *bwana*,' said Benny softly. 'Their cries have brought him.'

Hyram nodded in agreement.

'So what are we waiting for, then?' he snapped. 'Let's get after him.'

The three men melted into the smoke, leaving the Land Rover to its final, hissing death-throes.

The herd was completely silent now.

The fire had spread inexorably through the enclosure, gradually driving the elephants back to the horns of Cattle Rock, to where they had been brought in. Aunt Emily had taken charge and ushered the herd into the narrow rock corridor. But it was only a pretence of control, for the mood of the herd was beyond organization. In reality fear had moved their feet, fire had chosen their direction.

Now they milled around in the narrow, rock-bounded passageway, staring forlornly at the truck which blocked the exit, but with no thought of what to do.

Aunt Emily had taken her accustomed place at the rear of the herd. She tried to shield them from the intense heat pouring into the corridor from the enclosure by positioning her great body at the entrance. But heavy smoke still rolled in to choke them, and blasts of hot air funnelled in to sear their lungs.

In the way of all species, the females had gathered their young together and surrounded them in final, desperate attempts at survival, at preservation of the herd.

The new-born calf lay, gasping for breath, at his mother's feet. His tiny chest heaved with effort as he tried to suck oxygen from the depleted, acrid air. Cleopatra stood over him, her front legs straddling his body, her great bulk vainly trying to shield him from harm. Her trunk dangled limply from her lowered head. In her last moments her thought was only for her calf. The soft tip of her trunk gently caressed his face, calming the final, terrifying minutes of a life barely yet begun. The calf whimpered softly to himself.

The others seemed now beyond thought. Gradually they ceased making any movement. Each animal became still as it turned in upon itself to face its lonely end.

Emily groaned briefly, overcome with the heat. Her legs buckled and she slumped heavily onto the ground. Desperately she tried to rise again, pushing hard with her front legs. It was no use. Almost asphyxiated, she had no strength left. Her legs scraped and rasped vainly against the rock, then became still.

Slowly her great head sank down on to her front legs, and the life-light began to dim in her eyes.

Finally only Daffodil, on the threshold of maturity, the bull's battle-impulse almost fully formed, made a last effort.

Limping up to the truck he placed his head against its side and pushed. The truck moved slightly, but immediately settled again, rocking jerkily on its hard springs. Daffodil grunted with pain as the effort of pushing jarred his damaged leg. He pushed again. The same thing happened, but this time the leg gave way. He lurched sideways and slumped to the ground, defeated by his injury. He dragged himself disconsolately to his feet, stared miserably at the truck for a moment or two, then swung round and walked back to the herd.

His was now the only movement. The rest of the elephants stood, still as stones, in final recognition that the end had come.

As Daffodil approached he announced his failure to them in a long, despairing bellow; a screech of anguish and anger which echoed ringingly from the rocks. It bounced from wall to wall, pealing the death-knell of the ancient herd.

And, from outside, from beyond the rock walls, with a great bellow of rage and reassurance and challenge, the cry was answered.

'I'm here!' roared Papa Tembo.

Hearing him, every head lifted.

Hope had returned.

Laurens van der Wel sat with his back against a rock a few metres from the truck. He watched as the elephant within the enclosure tried to push the heavy vehicle out of the way. He smirked at the futility of it.

It was of little interest anyway. The herd had served its purpose. Papa Tembo was here. Close by. He could feel him approaching. The air itself was heavy, charged like a building thunderstorm with his presence. It was only a matter of time before he appeared.

The elephant abandoned its attempt to move the truck and van der Wel listened to the animal's feet shuffling away. He shrugged. It would have made no difference if it had escaped. He would have shot it in the stomach. Its dying screams might have brought Papa Tembo to him a little sooner, that's all.

And there was no hurry. He'd waited, after all, for fifty years. What was another few minutes?

He checked the safety catch for the hundredth time. It was off. As he had known.

He smiled to himself. He had been disappointed about the smoke, angered at the protection it gave to Papa Tembo. But now, wryly, he acknowledged its appropriateness. The bull was an old enemy. An old hatred. Picking him off while he was sleeping under a tree or grazing would, ultimately, have been without satisfaction. But this now was a challenge worthy of both of them. This was a battle of two cunning minds, played out in half-blindness, where swirling smoke gave advantage to each and the redness of the setting sun threw shadows profound enough to swallow man or elephant.

True, the elephant had some advantage. He could smell a man out, or hear him breathe.

But the decider in the end, and Laurens van der Wel smiled again as he thought of it, was the gun.

Papa Tembo could shift around at will; could, ghost-like, appear and vanish.

But eventually he would make a mistake.

The gun would never tire. It could shoot a thousand shadows, kill a thousand shifting smoke-clouds.

And eventually one of them would be Papa Tembo.

Behind him, the elephant who had pushed the truck trumpeted his disappointment.

And, in answer to his call, a great roar of rage rattled out from the depths of the smoke.

Papa Tembo.

Adrenalin coursed through Laurens van der Wel's body. He scrambled to his feet and lurched hurriedly away from the rock entrance, heading out into the smoke towards the sound. He stopped about twenty metres from the hill and listened.

No sound now.

His eyes prickled uncomfortably as he stared into the smoke, trying to read it with his mind, casting his senses out like a fisherman casting a fly. He strained his ears.

Nothing but the soft drum of the fire behind him.

But Papa Tembo was there. Just beyond his vision.

Everywhere and nowhere.

Van der Wel could smell him, could sense his soft feet brushing the grass, could feel his hatred hanging on the air.

Laughing, van der Wel swung his gun round at waist height and fired a volley of shots off to the left, to where the setting sun, huge and crimson, balanced on the rim of the world and poured long, liquid shafts of blood-red light into the smoke. Keeping his finger on the trigger he swung his body round through a hundred and eighty degrees, the bullets rattling out in a continuous deadly stream.

'Seek him out!' he screamed at the bullets as he swung through the murderous arc, emptying the cartridge at nothing.

But his voice died away and his finger eased off the trigger.

He froze and stared in disbelief. He felt his hands begin to tremble on the gun stock.

To his right, on the eastern horizon, the impossible, the unbelievable.

A second sun, huge and crimson, was setting on the other rim of the world.

A second sun.

The mythic symbol of ultimate dusk.

The apocalypse.

The end of all things.

And slowly, as he watched, into the huge blood-red orb, shot through with wisps of swirling smoke, the black and massive silhouette of the great bull began to appear. Distorted by prisms of shifting light, the shape seemed as huge as the sun itself.

Laurens van der Wel whimpered instinctively with irrational fear. Saliva began to dribble from his open mouth and run down his chin. He removed a hand from the gun and wiped his mouth nervously. He watched in incredulous disbelief as slowly, slowly the great bulk of Papa Tembo slid across the sun.

A vast, enchanted magic show, surreal in its immense proportions. A colossal, primeval shadow of the greatest beast on earth, cast huge, backlit upon a cosmic spotlight.

Van der Wel felt the hair rise on the back of his neck. Unwillingly, he began to turn towards the other horizon, reluctant to allow that what he saw might be true.

There, on the other rim of the world, the symbol was horribly complete.

A figure was crossing the other setting sun. A silhouette of a young, slender girl, walking with purpose.

As though she had an appointment at the end of the world.

Laurens van der Wel shuddered.

The Child of Man, the symbol of all mankind, the embodiment of all life was, as the Africans had foretold for millennia, appearing for the last time.

Now, as the two dying suns sank into the edges of the world, the earth would shrivel and all would die.

It was, of course, only a trick of the light. A strange freak of refraction, where a second, phantom sun was projected on to a wall of smoke.

Yes, that was it.

Van der Wel laughed nervously. The apparent reality of what he had seen had been startling, unnerving. Had made him doubt his senses.

He shook his head to clear it.

'Pull yourself together!' he snarled.

Obviously his imagination was playing tricks on him. The elephant was out there. There was no doubt about that. But a child walking about out there too. That was preposterous, fantastic, the figment of an over-anxious brain.

'Now, calm down,' he muttered.

He snapped out the empty cartridge clip and dropped it on the ground. He pulled a replacement from his top pocket and engaged it in the gun.

He felt better immediately. The everyday action of reloading his gun reassured him.

'Now,' he whispered, turning back to the eastern horizon, 'I'm ready for you.'

He began to rationalize things.

It was obvious what had happened. The elephant's shadow had been picked up by the real setting sun and projected on to the phantom one.

Van der Wel turned back again to the west.

That was where the elephant was, approaching from the west, coming directly out of the sun as any hunting animal would do.

He cocked his head to one side and listened intently.

Yes. There he was.

Sluff. Sluff. Sluff. Sluff.

Great feet approaching swiftly, emerging from the reddened depths of shadowed smoke.

Van der Wel raised the gun to his shoulder.

This was it. The moment for which he had waited half a century.

This was the repayment for all the years of shame and torture and bitterness.

The smoke swirled and shifted. Shapes moved within it as the heavy light of sunset stained the shadows.

Van der Wel's finger increased its pressure imperceptibly on the trigger.

There must be no mistake.

Time slowed as van der Wel's eyes darted this way and that, searching, searching.

And then . . . he began to appear. Indistinct at first, a moving smoke-cloud, but quickly clarifying, the great head emerged from the shifting mists.

Van der Wel's heart leapt in his chest as Papa Tembo appeared finally in his sights. Taking only the briefest aim he let out a great whoop of joy and yanked on the trigger. The automatic responded instantly, releasing a hail of bullets in a deadly, venomous stream at the great beast's head.

But in the split second before van der Wel pulled the trigger, something happened.

Something beyond comprehension.

A girl – *that* girl – emerged from the smoke, running at great speed. Before van der Wel could even register what was happening, she had hurled herself at him with such force that she unbalanced him.

He staggered, the gun jerked skyward and the bullets went raking uselessly up into the air.

Missing the elephant.

Missing Papa Tembo.

Laurens van der Wel gave a great howl of rage, the desperate disappointed scream of an animal cheated of its prey. He watched in disbelief as the elephant veered away, apparently unharmed, and vanished once again into the smoke. Instinctively he swung around, trying to dislodge his attacker. His right arm lashed out, hitting the girl hard on the side of her head. She screamed, staggered several paces with the impact, and fell to the ground.

Van der Wel gazed at her.

He shook his head, baffled at the turn of events, trying to make sense of things.

Where in heaven's name had this girl come from?

He stepped closer and stared at her. She lay gasping for breath, still stunned by the impact of the blow.

She whimpered as van der Wel loomed over her.

There was another noise from the smoke.

Startled, van der Wel swung round.

Shapes were moving in the swirling greyness.

He stared hard.

Men. The emerging shapes were men. The people the Mchawi had seen approaching. As he watched they were swallowed again by the smoke.

A cold, consuming rage at their interference flooded through him. They were spoiling everything. Here, at last, after half a century of waiting, his opportunity had come.

And had been spoiled.

His eyes moved back again to the figure lying on the ground.

Papa Tembo would have been dead now if she had not interfered.

'So,' he breathed. 'The Child of Man, are you?' He stared with icy fury at her. 'Perhaps,' he hissed.

He pressed the gun against the girl's temple.

'Well, girl, let's finish the story, shall we? For you, it *is* the end of the world.'

He increased the pressure on the trigger.

'And I, Laurens van der Wel, am the instrument of its end.'

'Jeez,' said Hyram.

The men emerged from the smoke.

Alison, almost unconscious with terror, saw them come.

'Help me!' she screamed. 'Oh, please help me.'

Benny was the first to take in the scene, the first to comprehend the strange tableau silhouetted against the red glow. The first to make sense of what this nightmare figure was about to do.

He leapt forward immediately, raised his gun to his shoulder and released a shot.

There was a scream of pain. The man whirled round and fell to the ground.

'Well done, Benny,' said Mike. 'Now, quickly, get to that girl.'

They began to run forward.

But immediately stopped in their tracks.

With a terrible, prolonged howl of fury and pain, Laurens van der Wel had rolled over onto his stomach and jammed the muzzle of the gun hard up against the girl's back.

'Get back!' he screamed. 'Get away!'

Benny raised his rifle again.

'Don't!' screamed van der Wel. 'Or I'll blow a hole in this girl that you could put your arm through. Back off! *Now!*

He waited until the men had retreated, then, keeping the gun firmly against the girl's back, he pushed himself up, by one arm, onto his knees. His face was contorted into a terrible, inhuman mask of rage and defiance.

The bullet had torn a gaping hole in his upper arm and shoulder and his beard and hair were spattered with blood from the wound.

But he was far from defeated.

He lurched to his feet, then, though the pain must have been beyond any human endurance, he bent down and hauled Alison up with his shattered arm. She screamed in terror as the arm, slimy with the warm wetness of his blood, locked around her throat and the barrel of the gun was rammed against her temple.

'Jeez,' said Hyram again. 'What in hell do we do now?'

He turned to find that two more men had emerged noiselessly out of the smoke.

'Alison!' the younger of the two shouted, and began to run towards her.

'Whoa,' said Hyram, intercepting him. 'Slow down, boy.'

'What in God's name . . . ?' said John Blake, trying to assess the situation.

'Stand still!' Mike ordered, sharply.

Van der Wel began to back away. Alison had gone limp with fear. Her feet trailed along the ground as the desperate man hauled her towards the truck.

The men could only watch in helpless anguish as the girl was dragged, like a rag doll, away from them and back into the deepening shadows.

Inch by painful inch they began to recede from view, to be swallowed by the gathering darkness.

And, barely perceptibly, as though it were being painted on to the backdrop, formed out of the profoundness of the dusk shadows, the huge, dark shape of Papa Tembo began to grow behind them.

They were backing straight towards him.

Van der Wel stopped and stiffened.

For a moment he remained motionless, puzzled.

A slow, dawning comprehension began to seep into his eyes.

There was a long pause.

Then, making his decision, van der Wel pushed Alison violently away from him. She staggered a couple of paces, fell to the ground and remained there, motionless.

The elephant took a step forward, then became still again.

Slowly, very slowly, van der Wel turned to face Papa Tembo, raising his gun as he turned.

His wounded arm dripped blood onto the grass.

Perhaps he knew it was the end. Perhaps the raising of the gun was only a gesture, one he knew to be futile, but one a man who had lived all his life by the gun would feel the need to make as he faced his life's end.

Papa Tembo's great trunk hissed casually through the air as the man turned. It caught van der Wel's arm just below the elbow, snapping it as though it were a twig.

The watching men heard the hiss and the sickening crack of bone. The gun fell from van der Wel's hand. He staggered with the force of the impact.

He remained hunched for a long time, his body twisted, convoluted with pain.

The elephant regarded him silently, impassively.

Incredibly, van der Wel recovered enough to pull himself erect and to his full height again. He stared directly at the elephant, as though defying him to beat him into submission.

Papa Tembo rumbled softly. His great trunk rose

and fell again, this time crashing down onto the man's collarbone.

Van der Wel was smashed to his knees by the force of the blow. But he made no sound. Not so much as a gasp or grunt of pain.

He remained on his knees for long minutes, breathing heavily, his shattered arms hanging uselessly at his sides.

The man and the elephant regarded each other, ancient hatreds feeding their stare.

Laurens van der Wel's mind went back for the last time to that fateful day when they had first met.

Perhaps Papa Tembo's did too.

Perhaps they both heard again the sounds of that day, echoing in their minds down half a century of years.

Perhaps here in their final meeting they both knew that they had been made by their memories. That they were what they were because of each other.

Now it was time to lay the ghosts to rest.

Papa Tembo's trunk raised again, high, high in the air. His vast bulk, prehistoric in size and strength, loomed over Laurens van der Wel, dwarfing him.

The watchers held their breath.

And even in his last seconds van der Wel could not release himself from hatred and contempt.

He raised his face up to Papa Tembo.

'Damn you!' he whispered. 'Damn you, and all your kind.'

The elephant stepped forward and the trunk whooshed down through the air.

This time it was not the casual action he had used to snap van der Wel's bones. This was the death blow, with all the unimaginable force that this most powerful of all earth's animals can summon.

There was a terrible, dull thump as Laurens van der Wel was smashed mercilessly into the ground, every bone in his body shattered into pieces by the immense violence of the blow.

The watching men gasped. The sound hit them in their chests as though they had been punched.

Papa Tembo surveyed the body perfunctorily then, deciding the job was done, stepped past it to where Alison lay. He stood at her side, reached out his trunk and, with infinite gentleness, touched her face.

The girl, almost insensible with the terror of her ordeal, was unable to move.

Snuffling gently, the velvet trunk explored the length of her body, as though searching for injury, touching her with great delicacy and sensitivity. Then, satisfied, the bull placed one foot against her side, rolled the girl against the foot to gain purchase and lifted her by her waist. She hung limply in his trunk, tiny and fragile, dwarfed by his immensity.

The men made to move forward.

Papa Tembo rumbled once. The men stopped. Not from fear. It was not a rumble of threat but of reassurance.

The bull turned away and began to walk towards the hill. The men followed at a distance.

As the dark shape of the truck began to loom out of the shadows the bull veered off. He walked to a point some metres to the side of the truck and then laid Alison gently down on the ground. He backed away several steps, then turned and looked at the approaching men. Immediately John Blake and Matt ran forward, dropped onto the ground and gathered Alison up in their arms.

Hearing Papa Tembo's approach, the trapped herd, huddled now right up against the body of the truck, began to call faintly.

'Quickly!' said Hyram. 'The truck.'

'I know, I know,' snapped Mike, already running towards the vehicle.

He leapt onto the central hub of the front wheel and swung himself up to open the cab door.

'The keys are in!' he shouted with relief, and slid immediately into the driver's seat.

The elephants started to jostle and push against the truck, as though willing it to move, assisting it on its way.

Mike turned the key and the engine clattered into life. He crashed the gear lever into first, lurched forward a few feet, then rammed it into reverse and shot back. He repeated this manoeuvre several times, easing the big, heavy machine round until, gradually, a gap started to open between the truck and the rock walls.

As the gap increased so did the volume of the calls. Almost at once the first of the elephants began to appear, pushing the back of the truck urgently as it came.

The young bulls, Boxer and Hamlet, were the first to force themselves out. Drugged by smoke and lack of oxygen they seemed disorientated and slow. But freedom gave them strength and they bellowed loudly. The young females followed quickly, rushing out past the truck and vanishing quickly into the gathering darkness.

A limping Daffodil came next.

Then Cleopatra emerged, with her tiny, baffled calf trotting earnestly at her heels. He staggered, weak with the smoke and the heat, but recovered quickly and managed to keep up with her.

Finally the remaining adult females shuffled out, peered momentarily around in dazed wonderment and began to walk slowly away. For a second they paused, looking back over their shoulders, knowing that one of their number remained, knowing they were incomplete.

But the figure they were seeking did not appear and they turned and walked away into the smoke.

Papa Tembo stood rock-still, implacably watching them go, registering no emotion, head raised, alertly assessing any further danger.

Soon it was over.

The sluffings of feet whispered away. Mike switched off the engine of the truck.

The fire, contained within the rock boundaries of the hill, was now beginning to burn itself out. Starved of grass to consume, its roar had diminished to a faint, smouldering hiss. That, Alison's soft sobbing, and her father's reassuring murmurs were soon the only sounds.

The great bull remained where he was, silent and motionless.

Mike rejoined Hyram and Benny. They too became silent.

There was nothing to say.

They stood, people and animal, each watching the other carefully, a few metres apart in space but a universe apart in spirit and species.

And the wonder of the miracle that had happened here was apparent to them all.

Man and animal had somehow come together; had been bonded briefly by a common need.

Papa Tembo continued to regard them. For long, long minutes he stood.

Waiting, it seemed.

Only when Alison had stopped sobbing and lay still and composed in her father's arms did the animal seem satisfied.

Only then did this most strange and mysterious of all the beasts of earth finally break his silence and stillness.

He gave a low, protracted rumble and began to move. He turned, and his soft feet took him silently away.

Soon his massive frame had melted into the shadows and he was gone.

EPILOGUE

'In my end is my beginning.'

T.S. Eliot, *East Coker*, 1940

They prepared to leave just after dawn. The fires had died, the smoke dispersed, the animals gone.

What remained of Laurens van der Wel's body they left where it was. Trampled by the fleeing herd it was hardly recognizable anyway.

'Shouldn't we bury him?' Benny asked.

'Wouldn't waste my strength,' said Hyram.

'Hmm,' said Mike in agreement.

And that, as far as everybody was concerned, was that.

Within a day the body was gone, vanished, without so much as a stain of blood left behind.

Within a week the first shoots of new grass began to fight their way up through the scorched earth of Cattle Rock.

Later a legend would arise that no grass would grow where Laurens van der Wel had died.

It wasn't true.

Just a story.

But this was true.

No elephant would ever pass the spot where this evil man had lain without stopping, without staring in suspicion at the place, without skirting round it, head raised, the whites of its eyes showing in anger.

And this too was true.

A year later, when lives had returned to normal, Alison Blake sat on a hillside overlooking a waterhole, watching the herd bathe and play.

Suddenly, without any warning, almost as though on a signal, the herd fell silent.

One by one they left the water, walked out into the open and stood staring at the horizon.

The entire herd. Just standing and staring.

It was at that moment, Alison knew, that Papa Tembo's long life had come to a close.

Somewhere, far out beyond the rim of the world, his last and loneliest journey had just reached its end.

Alison cried gently for him and the horizon blurred with her tears.

But tears do not last, for man or beast.

Quickly tiring of standing in a vigil he did not understand, Cleopatra's calf broke away and started to chase his tail.

Alison watched him and smiled.

Things happen, things continue.

'*Aia*,' whispered Alison, softly.

So be it.

'Like immortal flowers they have drifted down to us on the ocean of time, and their strangeness and beauty bring to our imaginations a dream and a picture of that unknown world, immeasurably far removed, where man was not: and when they perish, something of gladness goes out from nature, and the sunshine loses something of its brightness.'

W.V. Hudson, *The Naturalist in La Plata*, 1892

'The elephant is a vermin. He destroys crops and frightens villagers. The only answer is to utilize him or kill him.'

Peter Musavaya (ranger in Zimbabwe), 1996